Lorraine Marwood has published several children's novels and collections of poetry, winning the inaugural Prime Minister's Literary Award for children's fiction in 2010 for her novel *Star Jumps*. She has enjoyed three fellowships with the May Gibbs Children's Literature Trust. Her 2018 verse novel, *Leave Taking*, was the joint winner of the NSW Premier's Literary Awards, Patricia Wrightson Prize for Children's Literature and was shortlisted for the 2019 CBCA Book of the Year, Younger Readers and the Queensland Literary Awards, Children's Book Award. She lives in regional Victoria.

www.lorrainemarwood.com

First published 2021 by University of Queensland Press
PO Box 6042, St Lucia, Queensland 4067 Australia
Reprinted 2022 (twice)

University of Queensland Press (UQP) acknowledges the Traditional Owners and their custodianship of the lands on which UQP operates. We pay our respects to their Ancestors and their descendants, who continue cultural and spiritual connections to Country. We recognise their valuable contributions to Australian and global society.

uqp.com.au
reception@uqp.com.au

Cover design by Jo Hunt
Cover illustration by Kate Wong
Author photograph by Gingerhouse Photography
Typeset in 12/15 pt Adobe Garamond by Post Pre-press Group, Brisbane
Printed in Australia by McPherson's Printing Group

The University of Queensland Press is assisted by the Australian Government through the Australia Council, its arts funding and advisory body.

A catalogue record for this book is available from the National Library of Australia.

ISBN 978 0 7022 6283 8 (pbk)
ISBN 978 0 7022 6414 6 (epdf)
ISBN 978 0 7022 6415 3 (epub)
ISBN 978 0 7022 6416 0 (kindle)

University of Queensland Press uses papers that are natural, renewable and recyclable products made from wood grown in well-managed forests and other controlled sources. The logging and manufacturing processes conform to the environmental regulations of the country of origin.

FOOTPRINTS ON THE MOON

LORRAINE MARWOOD

UQP

To the memory of my own dear grandmother
and her beautiful garden.

Also dedicated to Vietnam veterans, many who braved
conscription in an unpopular war.

APRIL 1969

How to take a moon step

It seems to me
that I am taking
my own moon steps
about the same time
humans want
to conquer the moon.
I heard on my sister's radio
about President Kennedy's promise
to have a man on the moon
before the end
of the 1960s.
It's going to come true.
It really is, and
we might watch it,
watch history happening!

Will our world,
my world, suddenly change?
Will the moon I look at
every night
suddenly disappear?

'Cas?' I ask.
'Will the moon change colour
or grow antennas when
man lands on the moon?'

I am teasing Cas but part
of me is a bit worried.

'Don't be silly, Sharnie.'
My big sister laughs.
'You think about the strangest
things; there's more happening
around us than in outer space.'

Hmm. Really? I think
maybe Cas needs to look up
more often, try imagining
moonwalking, like me.

Lewis, our cousin
would agree.
He'd love to practise
moonwalking.

At night
I moon-gaze
when I put Jules,
my cat,
outside.
The silver
of a moonbeam reflects
along the length
of Jules's tail,
like a special wish.

If that moonbeam
caught me in its
glistening light,
what would I
wish for?

I want things
in my world
to stay the same,
but I want to learn
and make
new friends also.
Just like the moon
on its travels
around Earth
its changes
are shadowed,
halved and quartered
till it's full
and round again.

I don't know enough
about my little world
without stretching
my neck, my mind,
to look up at that speck,
in the turquoise night.
I imagine man
as a smaller

conquering speck
trampling on its
milky surface.

School is still an unmapped territory

I tiptoe
into my high school,
alien,
just like moon
exploration.

Even though it's April
everything's still new,
like the first day
at the beginning of the year:
subjects,
corridors,
lockers,
assemblies,
house colours,
books,
teachers,
rules.

Rules
written and unwritten
are the hardest to learn.

My sister, Cas,
already
aware of the rules,
keeps her distance.

Four years age
difference
seems like light-
years apart,
like an alien
force field
keeps us
orbiting
each other,
spinning
on our own
separate axis.

She is surrounded
by a group of friends;
they laugh,
tell jokes,
admire my sister's new
hairstyle
and her long legs.

I wave to Cas
and her friends
but none of them look
at little-sister me.

Not like last year
at primary school –
Cas would wait for me
at the school gate,

one of her friends
would carry my schoolbag
if I had an extra project
or artwork as well.

Cas would ask me about
my day, my teachers,
my friends, say,
'How was today, Sharnie?
Learn something new?
Find a new book to read?'

But now
she rarely asks anything,
and when I hold up
my latest library book
her eyes aren't
even focused
on me.

Friends and foes

I'm gobbled up in a
crazy jam of students
streaming to class,
all racing to lockers,
from lockers,
knocking into each other,
calling to friends,
shouting,
until Mia appears
at the mouth
of the long,
straight corridor.

Only a few of my old
primary classmates
came to the same
high school as me.
And I'm so glad
Mia is one.
As I watch, she is like
a flash of light
in a space telescope
weaving her way
against the flow
of students
as she comes
towards me

growing larger,
brighter
and her smile
growing with her.

We look up our first class
for the day
on the noticeboard
timetable: Science,
then Geography.
We pull faces and laugh.
Our least favourite subjects …

but we're not prepared
for the wonder ahead –
space possibilities
looking up, up,
not at our earthbound feet.

'So it's 1969,'
begins Miss Campbell
our Science teacher.
'Duh!' whispers Ellie,
loud enough for her friends
to giggle.
'And NASA is on course
to win the Space Race
for the USA,'
continues Miss Campbell
not fazed by Ellie.

‘Any idea how many people
have been involved
in this project
over the decade?’

‘One thousand,’ pipes Ellie again.
Miss Campbell merely smiles.
‘Two thousand,’ says Mia.
‘More,’ encourages Miss Campbell.
Silence.
‘Well, think of this number,’ says
Miss Campbell in a dramatic voice
as if she’s about to unwrap
a special birthday present.

‘Four hundred thousand
scientists and engineers,
worked for the American
aerospace program
leading up to now.’
‘And astronauts,’ adds Ellie,
to a chorus of giggles.
Phew! ‘That’s a lot,’
I whisper to Mia.

‘They worked day and night,’
went on Miss Campbell.
‘It was indeed
a space race of sorts,

trying to beat
the Russian Space Program.'

'Communists,' mutters Ellie
and pokes Marg,
who passes the word along
until it reaches the front row.
Miss Campbell nods.
'Yes, Communism
and the Cold War.'

'Now, Ellie,
why is this a Cold War?'
asks Miss Campbell.

'Because it's not armed warfare
like the Vietnam War but full
of sneaky things like beating
another country in the Space Race
and spying,' answers Ellie.

'Yes ...' agrees Miss Campbell slowly.
Marg gives Ellie a little
congratulatory hand clap.

Cold, I wonder,
like the moon?
Will the moon be cold?
Just like night-time,

blanketed
from the sun.

I wonder aloud
about the distance
of the moon from Earth,
wonder about
world powers
out to conquer space,
wonder about romance
and moon cheese.

Mia laughs about
the last part –
that the moon
is made of cheese.
We make up jingles
about the whey-
coloured moon,
about romance
and moonlight.
We sing softly
to each other,
giggle. Hands
shielding us
from prying eyes
and stopping the noise
reaching the front
of the room.

Ellie turns around
in her chair
and stares,
then pokes
Marg again
and whispers,
'Mia and Sharnie
love nursery rhymes,
little babies –
"little babies"
pass it on.'

Singing silly jingles
is not for high school.

So we whisper about
a newspaper cutting
of space food
the astronauts might eat:
dried food, baby food,
just add water,
and we laugh and think
of gravity, of lunch
floating by.

How close is our neighbour?

Next lesson is Geography
and Miss Parkes begins
by unfurling a huge map
along the chalkboard.
'What country is this?'
she asks.
I nudge Mia but she
has no idea.
We just seem to know
where Australia is,
and New Zealand
and England
and America.

'It's Vietnam,' begins Gail,
a classmate I hardly know.
'Yeah! Communists
want to take it over,'
adds Ellie in a shrill voice.

'Yes,' agrees Miss Parkes,
and she begins to tell
us about South Vietnam
and the communist North
and how Australia, with America,
is advising and training
the South Vietnamese army.

Miss Parkes hands out sheets
with a map of Vietnam.

I can see Gail squirming
in her seat
wanting to say something,
but Miss Parkes ignores her
and starts to write
on the chalkboard.

For homework
Where is Saigon?
Who is Ho Chi Minh?
Who are the Vietcong?
What country formerly ruled Vietnam?
Why is there a war happening
between the South and North?

Ellie makes sure everyone hears
her repeat the words,
'Communist takeover'.
The bell rings and
we stream
out of class.

Listening with her heart

I visit Grandma
after school.
Cas used to come
with me,
but not now,
not this year,
not lately.

Grandma doesn't
live far away;
I just have to
walk across
our street,
through a little
park of patchy grass,
turn the corner and
it is the second
house, a big
block with trees.

I lift the catch on
Grandma's gate –
already the sweet peas
and roses
reach out to me
with their rich perfume.

I zigzag across
the mosaic
of pavers,
trying not
to touch the join
between each one.
With each step
I'm kinda praying:
Keep Grandma
safe today,
today,
safe today.

I can tell her everything:
what high school's really like,
how I worry about
not knowing
what I really want to do
with my life.

I even tell my grandma about
the shows I watch on telly,
my favourite songs,
and how the moon
is starting to feel closer now.
I ask her about being brave,
about how the astronauts
must be brave
to go somewhere

like the moon.
What if they don't come back?

My grandmother
smiles through all of this,
sometimes holds my hand,
nods her head,
listens to me the way
no one else does.

We sip a fresh pot
of tea, brewed
in the battered
silver teapot,
and drink from her delicate
rose-entwined teacups.
I bite into Grandma's
rich, homemade
chocolate slice
and later her sticky
peanut brittle.

Then it's my turn to sit
while Grandma talks,
but it's like she's caught
in the same script.
She tells me again
about the making
of peanut brittle.

Again and again she says,
'Watch out, it might burn.'

When I look
at the back of her hand
I see a red welt,
a burn mark.
'Oh! Your hand!' I say,
as I jump up to find
something to put
on that welt.
'Does it hurt?' I babble,
looking for the aloe vera plant
Grandma has growing
with her herbs.
She has been
teaching me about herbs
when I visit.

But she doesn't look
at the welt.
Instead, she surprises
me by placing her
arms around me
and saying,
'Will I teach you
how to make peanut
brittle this weekend,
after the Anzac parade?

You know it was your
grandfather's favourite sweet.
We can remember him then.
Someone has to continue
the family recipe
when I'm gone.'

Grandma's peanut brittle
Do Not Stir
6 tablespoons of water
7 tablespoons of sugar
Boil on fast heat until golden brown.
In flat tin, put peanuts, pour toffee mixture
over the top and let it get cold.
Put in an airtight container (most important)
to keep it crackly.

I nod, trying not to look sad
and know deep inside
that something is wrong,
something is happening
to Grandma.

Then she smiles
and hugs me again.
'Maybe we could make
your own family food book.
Do a test run of each
recipe here?'
'Yes,' I hug her back;

she is again
the grandmother
I’ve always known.

Good morning America

Cas has a morning routine:
radio on, loud, when I'm
still stitched to my pillow
by sleep, my hair tousled
to cloud dreams.
I take time
to wake from the night's
hibernation,
but Cas is up, out
of her bed on the other
side of our room
as soon as the sun's watery
light washes through
the louvre slats
of our window.

'Turn it down,' I bear-growl,
but Cas is singing
as she brushes
her thick brown hair
deliberately blocking me out.

She stops singing
as the music switches
to the news.
'Protests have taken place
in America over the cost of the

space moon program.
“End poverty
on Earth first”
is the banner message.’

Cas turns the volume down,
not because I asked,
but because
she wants to say,
‘Of course they should
grow more food,
find more jobs,
stop the wars here
before they go
to the moon frontier.’
The hairbrush snags
on a knot,
‘Ouch,’ she hisses.
‘And America should stop
the war in Vietnam,’ she mutters
and flings the hairbrush
back on the dressing table.
It makes a loud thud.

I’m awake now and ask,
‘Vietnam? Since when did you
become interested in the war?
We are learning
about Vietnam in Geography.
But what’s it got to do with us

in this little town so far
away from the city?'

Cas opens her mouth
and looks at me.
I'm looking right back
wondering how Cas
knows more than I do
about the war
that's part
of our lessons,
complete with
a school project.

Then Peter Sarstedt
sings the song
'Where Do You Go To
My Lovely?'
and I don't wait
for Cas's reply.
I can't help singing it
and mouth all the lyrics
to myself as I push back
my quilt and open the louvres
to let in the fresh breeze.

Cas turns away,
finishes getting
ready for the day.
She squeezes lemon juice

on those
tanned smooth legs,
and I know
as she makes
her way to school
later that eyes
will flick,
heads
follow and even
a wolf-whistle
will be the reward
of her citrus
mornings.

When the song finishes
Cas looks at me.
'You'll be late,
won't have time
to do your hair
or clean your shoes.'

'You didn't care that much
about me yesterday at school,
you wouldn't even know
if my shoes were clean then,
so why worry about it now?'

And I wish I could throw
something down so it made
a great thwacking noise, too.

Missing Dad

'Moody,' Cas calls me.
'Sulky,' Dad often says.
'There's a little
man on your shoulder,'
he jokes
and goes to swipe it off.
Then stops, laughs
and begins to tell me
the story of how his mother
called him moody when
he was my age.
I like Dad's
stories and know 'the little
man' is his way
to shake me out
of my dreaming.
Or he might finish the story with:
'You'll never plough a field
by turning it over in your mind.'
That usually does the trick,
I can't see a plough in sight
and my mind,
is it really like a field?

I'm not moody, just trying
to work Cas out these days.
I think she's the one with

mood swings.
I feel like
I don't know
this
new
Cas.

Sulky? Nah!
Dad is away so much lately
that I'm unsure what to say
when he is here.
His work keeps him gone
a month at a time.
That's ages, it really is.
It's like I'm meeting
him again, like a long-
lost relative,
each time he comes
home.

He used to work on our little
block of land, all the time,
feeding the pens of chooks,
keeping two cows,
three pigs,
a few sheep,
lots of fruit trees
and a big veggie patch.
But selling eggs doesn't pay.
We would rather

store-bought milk
than straight from
our cows,
and keeping two
growing girls
costs a lot.
So, Dad took a job
selling farm goods
to places a long way
from here.

Maybe I see the man
in the moon
more than I do
my own dad.

Last year, Dad would read
me a serial; one time it was
The Princess and the Goblin,
another time *Grimm's Fairy Tales*.
He'd put on different voices
especially for the scary parts,
but now I'm a big
high-schooler
Cas says I'm too old
for a bedtime story.

But I still want stories,
lots of them
and time with my dad.

But there's Jules

I have a cat, a very
fluffy moccasin-slipper-
like cat.
'Shoo,' says Cas
if Jules tries to sneak
into our bedroom.
If we leave
the louvres
of our window
open just cat-width,
Jules will
curl like a seashell
on one of our
patchwork quilts.

This morning
I wish I could run
my feet over
Jules's soft back.
Instead, I switch off
Cas's radio and feel better.

I go to the bathroom,
wash my face
with cold water;
Jules follows.

I smell toast cooking,
hear the kettle
singing on
the wood stove
and hurry for hot Milo,
warm buttery
crunchy toast
and Mum's
good-morning smile.

But Mum's talking
on the phone,
the long black cord
jiggling as she
pulls it taut,
trying to cook toast
as well as listen.
Her hand stills,
her face creases,
and I know it's
my grandmother.

When she puts
down the receiver
I ask, 'What's wrong?
It's Grandma, isn't it?'
My voice catches
on the last word.

'Not now, Sharnie,
you'll be late for the bus.'
Mum is distracted,
Mum is keeping
Grandma from me.
'But—' I say.

'Ten minutes
and I'm walking,' calls Cas.
I know it takes us
longer than that
to walk to the bus stop.

Cas is in the bathroom,
again.
I wonder if the mirror
ever gets a chance to show
someone else's reflection.

I gobble the last
of my toast,
rinse my plate and mug,
look one last time
at Mum who is
buttering bread,
finding apples,
packing our lunches
as if everything is fine.

But it's not, it's not.
She's been talking
to Grandma,
listening, but not sharing
with me, with Cas.

I hate not knowing.
I'm not a child anymore.
I'm trying hard to be
a high-schooler,
more grown up.
I'm trying,
really trying.

History for real

Mia sits with me again,
a Vietnam continent
still splashed on the wall.
Miss Parkes is
pointing with a stick
to areas on the map
like Biên Hòa:
'Where the first
Australian battalion
served with American troops
under their command.
This was June 1965.'

'Biên Hòa,' Mia whispers,
and somehow
we find it funny
and our giggles
seep through
hands held
to our mouths
and come squeaking
and muffled
into the big
classroom.

We duck our
heads lower

but giggling
is like the measles:
contagious and makes
us red-cheeked.
We are laughing
for no reason,
but stop suddenly
when Miss Parkes
looks straight
at Mia and me
and says:
'So this is your Geography
report – very topical –
on the start and causes
of the Vietnam War.
Why is Australia
involved in this war?'

There are shuffling feet,
loud whispers
and hands shoot up
to ask questions.

'Hands down,'
says Miss Parkes.
'These questions are part
of your assignment.
You will need
to seek
answers yourselves,

read the newspapers,
look up the library's
encyclopedias.
I have written
a basic timeline here
on these sheets
and it will be your task
to fill in the gaps.

As the sheets are passed
from desk to desk,
Gail, sitting behind us,
taps me on the shoulder.
'What are you laughing at?
Are you laughing at me?'
she asks.
That only makes
me giggle more.
Ellie and her friend, Marg,
at the desk across from us
laugh too, but somehow
their expressions stop
my giggles. They are
smirking at Gail.

Did I look like that?
That horrible sneer
on Ellie's face?
Goading Gail, almost
as if she wants

Gail to fight back,
taunt back, hit back,
anything,
but Gail ignores her
and asks me
a question
that should have been
fired on Ellie.

'No, Gail,' I protest.
'I wouldn't laugh at you.
I'm sorry if you thought that.'
And my face flames red
as if I've been caught out
in a lie.

But it's true; I'm
not like Ellie,
not at all.
Even though we had
a fit of giggles,
I just don't laugh
at people.

I don't want to say
Gail is weird.
Different,
yes,
lonely,
yes.

How lonely,
I don’t know
until we are
in the next class.

Moon craters of our own

Miss Anders, of Social Studies fame
puts Simon & Garfunkel's
'I Am a Rock'
on the portable record player
she brought to the lesson.

'Are we individual rocks
or part of a group?
Are there times when
we feel like lone rocks?'

The music and words
are familiar to us all,
but Miss Anders makes
me think.

Mia giggles; I don't.
Ellie sort of snorts,
half-laugh,
half-growl.
It seems to be
a signal for the rest
of the class.
No one answers,
several girls cough,
some shuffle feet,
deliberately

knock a ruler
to the floor.

Gail speaks in a rush,
'It's good to be
an island sometimes.'

Ellie sniggers,
then Marg and some
of their other friends
sing softly, about Gail
being a rock,
on her own island
far, far away.
Miss Anders pushes
her glasses
up onto the bridge
of her nose
and tries to quieten Ellie
and her friends,
her arms waving
like seaweed,
to and fro.

But Ellie
guffaws and sings
even louder.

Gail drops her head
into her arms

on the desk,
and Miss Anders wails,
'Girls, *please*!'

I'm stunned, and think
about turning to Gail,
about thumbing my nose
at Ellie, but all I really do
is sit there and watch.
A little tsunami has just
washed over Gail's beach
and wet us through,
making me gritty
and uneasy.

I know I should do
something,
say something,
but I am just
like everyone
else in the class:
I leave Gail
to sink or swim.

Our own archeology of artefacts

The ringing of the bell
saves everyone.
The girls
are like trumpeting
elephants
storming for the door,
storming down
the corridor
to lockers and lunch,
until the principal,
Mr Grear,
calls them to stop
and serves
them a little homily.

Miss Anders, shuffling
through her notes,
packing up the portable
record player, looks up
and smiles weakly
at Mia and me. But
doesn't even offer
Gail a gentle word.

I think maybe we
are like rocks,
and Ellie and her friends

are like the sea smashing
at us, but mainly at Gail.

Mia and I go
to the small hill
near the hockey oval
at lunchtime.
It's quiet
and we're still
thinking of rocks.
The hill has lots
of rocks;
we pull and dig
and turn them over.
I find a little rock
with curvy lines through it
like chocolate melting.

'This would be good
for the treasures
Grandma puts in her pots,'
I say. Mia finds another
stone and hands it to me,
then she gets tired
of looking.
'Rocks, rocks, rocks,'
mutters Mia.

I ask,
'What's wrong with Gail?'

Mia doesn't know.
I say, 'Maybe Gail
is drowning.'
I'm suddenly serious,
and straightaway
I'm sorry
for those words.

Somehow, when I see Gail
I think of Grandma;
they are both flickering
on their own moonbeams
and I'm trying
to reach Grandma
but her light is
quickly going dim.

What we cherish

Last class for today
is Art and we are looking
for inspiration in ancient
monuments. We turn
the pages of our textbooks.
'Imagine storing lots
of things in pyramids
for your afterlife.'
Mia is pointing
to the fabulous
necklaces the
pharaohs wore,
but I'm thinking
of all those
slaves. Carrying,
carting, digging,
all for the future death
of the pharaoh.
'All those
hieroglyphics.
Wonder what
secrets they hide?'
I say.

Then, strangely,
I think of Grandma again
and wonder what

she would place
in her own pyramid.
She gathers treasure,
her own sort:
leaves, twigs,
glass, shells,
broken pottery;
they make squiggly
lines in her garden
and pot plants.
The pharaohs wouldn't think
of broken shards as treasure,
or even curly leaves
that would
moulder away.
But sometimes
Grandma has special
wonderful
pieces to keep safe.

Once Grandma let me
hold her most precious
glass ornament
in the china cabinet:
a red horse,
red tail flaming out,
prancing.

If I was
my younger cousin

Lewis,
I would say
it looked like
a horse that flew
too close to the sun.
An outer space,
alien horse,
but so beautiful.

Grandma
told me the story
of Grandpa
winning the ornament
at the local show.
'He had to shoot
all the tin ducks
as they floated across
the sideshow stall.
He never missed
a one.
I could have
had a huge teddy
bear, or a kewpie doll
on a stick, but that
horse, it shimmered.
And your grandpa
gave it to me with a kiss.
It was the day
he asked me
to marry him.'

And I think, *How*
come the red horse
is here, but not
my grandpa?
I can't remember
much about him,
but to me he is
as wonderful
as that ornament.

Mum told me
that she was barely
a teenager
when he died.
'Killed in action in
New Guinea,' she said,
'in the jungle there
and your grandma
worked so hard
to bring up
Aunty Jessy
and me. I can
remember seeing her
cry at the clothesline
one morning, just letting
the tears fall down
her cheeks unchecked,
and when she saw me,
she wiped the tears
away and said,

"Today is our
wedding anniversary."
Then went on pegging
the clothes on the line.'

Cas is full of surprises

Going home,
all Cas's friends get
off the bus
a stop before we do.
Cas sits
with an older boy,
holding hands,
bending
so that their
heads touch.
I heard Cas's friends
whisper that his name
is Tyson,
that he can't get a job,
has lots of time,
can wait for Cas after school,
can catch the bus with her
until his stop comes up.

'Back
from
Vietnam.'
I heard
that last whisper long
and hissing
like a snake.

Tyson seems to know
I'm studying him
and he looks across
at me and grins.
Cas looks up and sort
of grimaces, but Tyson
whispers in her ear
and they both look
down at their clasped hands.
That smile makes me like
Tyson and I realise
I want to know
more about him.

When the bus pulls
in at our stop,
I think that maybe Cas
isn't going to get off,
but she clamours
down the steps
and nudges me.
'Don't tell Mum.'

Cas and secrets,
Grandma and pyramids,
both saving and hiding
important events
from the world
around them.

Lewis, space walker

It's so clear
and quiet outside
but not inside
my head.
I think about today,
about rocks
and the moon,
also about Gail,
and I find myself
walking to Grandma's.

Ellie's sniggering
and taunting
comes back to me,
haunts me.
Deep inside I wanted
to do something,
stop Ellie,
but I was just like
Miss Anders,
helpless,
afraid.
Of what?
What Ellie might say?
What Mia might say?

I am shaking my head
and muttering to myself,
so when Lewis
appears before me,
with a space helmet
on his head,
I get a fright.

He's nearly nine
but knows so much
and surprises me
with all the schemes
and projects
he comes up with.
And sometimes
annoyingly,
he is always
going to Grandma's
when I am, too.

'What are you
doing here?' I ask.

He shrugs.
'Sometimes I don't go
to school and go
help Grandma
in the garden instead,
or she'll tell me stories

about Grandpa.
I learn more then anyway.'

'What?' I explode.
'Does your mum know this?'

'She's too busy working
at her cleaning jobs,
says it's hard
to keep money
coming in.'

'But Lewis, you're
too young
to miss school.'

'Nah! I can read
and write and do
astronaut maths,
that's all I need.
Besides, Grandma
doesn't mind,
she thinks it's
a Saturday
when I visit.

'And,' he says,
'it's only once a week
or not even that much.

Don't tell,' he pleads
as he turns big,
sorrowful eyes
right at me.

How many secrets
can I keep?
I used to think
the moon
was a secret.
Soon it won't be
anymore.

'What do you think
of my space helmet?' he asks,
changing the subject.

I look closer
and see it's just
a gouged-out watermelon,
all squished looking.
I try not to laugh.

'You look like a green-
and-red spotted alien,'
I say. 'And it will keep
you warm in winter,
if it lasts that long,' I add.
'Besides, you could dry
those black pips

and plant them
in Grandma's garden.'

He nods and
the helmet slides.
'I'm going to be an astronaut
when I grow up,' he says.
'Look!' He holds up
a whole roll of aluminium foil.
'For space boots,' he shouts,
and the thin whirr
of aluminium
fills the moon sky
as Lewis lets
the whole roll spill
across the lawn.

Memory is treasure, too

We haven't gone into
Grandma's yet,
but somehow I
think she might
not be home;
she would have heard
us by now.
Sometimes her next-door
neighbour takes her
to bingo
or for groceries.

I watch Lewis break
off foil for boots,
an ideal time to try
out some moon facts
on him.
After all, if he plans
to be an astronaut
then he needs
to know about the moon.

'Okay, Lewis:
Does the moon travel around
Earth in a circle?'

Lewis looks up at the sky,
a bit awkward in
his watermelon helmet.
'Nah, it's elliptical,
like an oval.'
I'm impressed,
smart little cousin.

Then Lewis does something
only Lewis
would do and breaks off
a piece of his space
helmet and squishes me
with watermelon juice.

'Shouldn't you go home?'
I splutter at him
as I try to wipe
off sticky juice
on my cheeks,
on my hands.

He just stands there
grinning,
so I add, 'Looks like
Grandma's not home anyway,
otherwise she'd
be out here admiring
your space outfit.'

Lewis nods carefully.
'Mum says it's fine
to be here.'

'It will be getting dark soon,'
I remind him.
'Your mum will
have your tea ready.'
Food always
seems to trigger
a response from Lewis.

'Okay, see you later,
over and out.'
And he scrambles
out the back gate
to his home a few
doors down.

I pick up several
of the black pips
with watermelon flesh
attached and think
about Lewis's mum,
my aunty Jessy,
how she struggles,
with my uncle Tom often
in a rehabilitation home
suffering still from his
injuries in the Korean War.

How wars still
roll on even when
they are officially
ended.
Then a new war starts.
Our family has notched
up enough memories
of battles over the years.
Now Cas is making
a connection with the war
our country is in
right now.

I wash the pips
clean under
the tap at Grandma's
front gate
and place them on
top of an upturned
flowerpot to dry
in the sun.

I turn to go home
myself
when something
makes me pause …
I just know
something
is wrong.

I hurry to the back door,
not caring where my
feet land. I slow
when I reach
the flywire door.
I knock quickly and call,
'Grandma, I'm here.'

A noise like
something breaking
comes from the kitchen.
I push the door handle
and let myself in.

Grandma looks up.
She is bending over.
'For you, Sharnie darling.'
I make a noise like a sob
when I see the fragments
of the tiny
red horse made of glass.

'I was getting it down,
ready to wrap
for you, Sharnie.
For you.'

Grandma's hair is tousled
as if she's
forgotten to brush it today,

her shirt is covered
with spots of egg dribble
and a stain like blood
spurts over
the lino.
'I want you to have
it now in case—'
Her words are breaking, too.

'Your hand,' I cry.
'It's cut.'
I race for a cloth,
then when Grandma
is seated and the kettle on
for a sweet cup of tea –
'I need fortifying,'
says Grandma –
I go to find Mum.

Mum runs back
with me to Grandma's.
'Just a little cut,' she soothes,
and motions
for me to sweep
up the broken pieces.
A little tear joins
the glass as the story
about Grandpa winning
and asking Grandma
to marry him

seems to fade
as I sweep away
the last of the red horse.

Cas, oh Cas

Later that night,
Cas eventually comes
into our bedroom.
I wait a while.
'Um, Cas?' I ask
as I look at her reflection.
She's trying out her hair
in pigtails,
then plaits,
putting in ribbons,
hairbands,
pushing in clips
and even trying
out her beanie
with the red pompom.
If I wasn't feeling so sad
I would laugh.

Cas looks away
from the mirror,
looks at me.
Perhaps I've somehow
sent an 'it's serious' message,
because she downs
her hairbrush,
puts the lid

on the hairspray.
'What's up, Sharnie?'

I plunge straight in.
'Umm, is there something
wrong if you start
forgetting things,
you know,
repeat what
you've just said?'

Cas says nothing,
so I keep on babbling.
'Because Grandma
is starting to forget …
to do silly things like …'

I shock myself
and Cas
when I feel the tears
slide down my face
and I really begin
to cry.

'Oh, Sharnie,' soothes Cas,
and she cuddles me.
'It's old age, just old age.
You can't expect Grandma
to live forever, you know.'

'Why not?' I gulp.
It's silly,
I know the answer –
well sort of –
but it feels good
with Cas's arms around me
and a little-sister question
to ask. I miss Cas being
this close, being all mine
for just a little bit.

All things lunar

The next day after school
Lewis comes with me
to visit Grandma.
'I have lunar dust.'
And he sprinkles me
with icing sugar.

'Yum, it tastes nice,' I say.
'There'll be no moon left,
soon we might eat it all up,'
he says, and laughs.

We are still giggling
as we push Grandma's
gate open. I look
quickly at the watermelon
pips and see they are drying.
Little garden pots
are lined up the length
of the front porch,
like tiny moon shoes.
'Hope Grandma
is feeling better today,'
I say to Lewis,
half-wish, half-prayer.

'Come in,' calls Grandma
as she cuddles us both.
'Your hand?'
I ask as I see the bandage.
'Yes, silly me. Just a small
cut, so sorry Sharnie,
about the red horse …'

'Want to help strike
some plants?' Grandma asks,
still holding us close.
Lewis shakes his head
and pushes away.
'Not unless it's a moon plant,'
he mutters.

'Well,' begins Grandma,
'your grandpa always
planted seeds or seedlings
according to the moon's phases.'

Lewis has a smile on his face.
'Really?' he asks
as if Grandma has just
found a piece
of moon particle for him.

'You know what phases are?'
she prompts.

‘Phases,’ replies Lewis,
‘are kind of like slices
of the moon that we see
night after night, until
the moon is whole again.’

‘Well done!’ laughs Grandma.
‘I couldn’t have
explained it better myself.’

‘Now here’s a chart
for this month’s
moon gardening.’

And Lewis is
totally drawn in,
his whole body
is still while he works
out today’s date
and looks up the phases
of the moon.

‘Full moon tonight,’
he shouts.
‘Yes, a good time
to transplant seedlings
or a plant
that needs root growth.’
‘Why?’ I ask.
‘Because the moon

is pulling moisture
to the top of the soil,'
answers Grandma.

Hmm, I think.
Really?

'By gravitation?'
asks Lewis.
Grandma nods.
'I don't know too much
about it all,
your grandpa was the one,
but I can teach you how
to strike some plants now,
like this lavender or—'
'Herbs?' I interrupt.
'Rosemary?'
'Why, yes, darling,
we can take a cutting now
from the rosemary bush.'

Grandma shows us
what to do,
and we have a go.

Our fingers
are gloves of soil
and we feel
like space magicians,

pulling new life
out of a little twig.

Grandma looks better,
sounds better,
almost like her old self.
But her right hand
is bandaged
and the pieces
of the red horse
are gone forever.
I wish I could place
a piece of the horse
in the new pot
I've just planted.
But I know I swept
up most of the pieces
I could see and put them
in the bin. I wasn't thinking
about saving them,
just thinking
of Grandma hurt.
Maybe I might find
a seed pod
to put there instead.

Grandma seems to know
what I am thinking.
'Come over here, Sharnie.
Choose from my container

of found objects, these
are what I've found lately
when I've gone
for a little walk.'

I follow Grandma and look
at her clay plant pots filled
with bits and pieces.
I've always loved these pots
and now I carefully sort
through one until
I find a curved piece of rock.

'Like a lemon slice
of moon,' I say and place
it in my pot with my cuttings
of lavender and rosemary.

Wars and remembering

On Friday,
it's Anzac Day
and Grandma, Lewis,
Mum and I
go to the shrine
in the town centre.
'A cenotaph,'
Grandma calls it.
I came with Grandma
last year
and the year before that,
but Mum usually stays
home. 'Too sad,' she said
last year, but today she comes.
She's worried about Grandma,
I know, we all are.

When Cas was asked
to come, she said,
'I don't think so,'
and that was that.
Dad comes when his work
allows it, but not this year.
Lewis's dad came
a year or two ago,
but Aunty Jessy says
it makes him too ill

afterwards,
all those painful
memories.

It's cold so early
in the morning
and there's only
a trickle of spectators,
but I love the way
the sun strikes
the granite of the shrine
and lights up
the little silvered
names of the men
who fought
and died
in the two world wars.

I squint as I look
at other wars listed:
Boer, Korean; always
wars in other countries
far away.

We watch the
returned soldiers
march.
Grandma points,
'That's Grandpa's mate,
he was in the same regiment;

that fellow over there
lost his arm
in an ambush …'
I can't quite hear
everything over
the boom
of the brass band,
but war sounds hard,
cruel,
full of pain.

A soldier stands
to attention
and I study him
to see how old he is:
more than eighteen,
and I think of Tyson.

Then I see Gail;
she is holding her
young sister close.
Her mother is there, too,
clutching Gail's arm
as if she might fall over
at any moment.
Gail doesn't look around,
just helps her sister
lay a wreath.
Her mother bows her head
as if saying a silent prayer.

I turn to Grandma,
she is watching them, too.
I wonder why they are here.
Maybe like us they are
honouring family members.
I don't see Gail's father, so
that makes me wonder
some more.

When it is our turn,
we climb the steps
side by side.
Lewis, Grandma and me
and Mum just a step behind.
We place our wreath.
My grandma
has attached
a little note:
For dear Herb,
I miss you so much.

I never knew my grandpa
so I think of him shooting
straight and accurately
to win a red horse,
not for anything more.
We stand for a minute's
silence as the bugle
plays its lonely tune.

Suddenly the silence
is broken by
some raised voices.

'Ban wars,
stop conscription!'

I see several posters
hoisted shoulder-high,
the ugly black-and-white
lettering and a graphic image
of barbed wire and guns.
Send our troops home!
Stop conscription now!

'Protestors!' says Grandma
and slowly nods her head.
'The last war didn't solve
anything. Will this war
stop conflicts and lead to
peace?
What about mothers
and wives and children …'
Her voice breaks
on those last words.
She tries to move closer
to the noise,
but is shaky
on her feet.

Mum takes her
gently by the arm
and talks soothingly
about Grandpa
and what a great
man he was,
so gentle.

Then something
catches my eye.
I'm not sure,
but Cas was trying
on a beanie
like the one I see
now on a protestor.
I'd know it anywhere
because it also has
a red pompom
that I sewed on top.

I don't tell anyone
about the beanie,
but on the way home
Lewis asks Grandma
about conscription.
'It's compulsory
military training for young
men turning twenty.
They then have

to do two years
full-time training
in the army.'
'They don't get a choice?'
Lewis asks.

'Their birthdate
goes into a ballot
and if that
number comes up
they don't have a choice.
Boys have to register
for national service,'
she tells us.
'Then suddenly
they become men
and have to be
willing to face death.
Wars,' mutters Grandma.
'I'd hate for my grandson
to be the first conscript
killed like that boy from
South Australia,
only child too …'

Her hands are cold
when I hold them
and her eyes
have a mistiness
about them.

I switch to asking about
cuttings, about flowers,
about baking
chocolate slice,
anything
but protestors,
war and Vietnam.

We walk Grandma back
to her gate. Mum takes
Grandma's arm, helps
her to the front
door, but Grandma turns
to me and whispers,
'If I were braver, I'd be
like Cas, too.'
She lifts her hand,
waves to Lewis and me
and moves away with Mum.

'What does Grandma mean?'
asks Lewis, as he knocks
the heads off
every flower we pass
on the way to his house.
'Got another Martian,'
he mutters as each head falls.
Lucky it's not
Grandma's garden,

I think.
'Nothing,' I say,
and Lewis believes me.

Where have you gone, Cas?

I think about Cas
a lot, especially after I saw
her in the school corridor
yesterday.
She was just standing
at her locker
by herself
staring,
just staring.
I wanted to ask her
about Tyson,
tell her that I think
he's okay,
but she didn't
look up;
her lips were
the shape of downturned
moon crescents,
her eyes were smudges
of moon dust.

'What's wrong, Cas?'
I wanted to hug her,
give her a little piece
of my happiness
to hang onto.
She looked at me then,

shook her head
and scrunched the heart-
shaped letter she was holding.
'Don't ask,'
her look seemed to say.

Now, we are in our bedroom
together and Mum
is still with Grandma and
of course
Dad is away in the country
somewhere.
I watch as Cas
pulls that heart-shaped letter
from under her pillow.

'Cas,' I begin, 'the Anzac parade,
were you marching in the protest?'
Cas swivels around
and her face
shows surprise,
then anger, then fear.
She scowls.
'None of your business, Sharnie.'

'But it is, Cas, it is! I'm
scared that Dad will
find out, that Mum will, too,
that they'll carry on.
You know how Dad

supports this war,
how it's the right
way to go!
Do you reckon Dad
will be happy knowing
you're a protestor?
Remember when he heard
about the school teacher
who refused to obey
his call-up papers
and was jailed?
He told us about Grandpa,
about his father and uncles
all fighting in the
First and Second World Wars?
How brave, how patriotic ...'

Cas slowly nods her head,
looks down at the letter
she is clutching.
Her face crumples a bit
and she's the Cas
I've always known.
'But it's not right, Sharnie,
this war.
They don't report things
in the paper or on the news.
They cover things up.
Tyson says—'
But Cas stops,

turns away,
then suddenly hisses,
'Don't you tell them anything!'

Seeking answers, so much to find out

I need to chat to Grandma,
maybe she can answer
my questions.
She might show me
Grandpa's medals
from the war,
talk to me about what
Grandpa might have said,
how she felt when
the war was raging.
I know Grandma thinks
a lot about the war
Grandpa was in,
the Second World War.

My life, now I'm at
high school,
seems so much bigger.
Maybe I'm taking
more notice
of things around me,
learning new subjects,
reading more books,
seeing new classmates,
listening to them talk.
And wanting
the world around

me to be fine –
no, not just fine –
happy.

On Sunday,
I plan a visit
to Grandma,
I want to see how
she is after
her stumble and confusion
at the Anzac service.

I go armed
with a notebook.
I want to write
down some of
Grandma's memories,
maybe use some
in my Geography assignment.
Well, that's what I tell myself,
but I'm frightened Grandma
is failing fast and my time
might be running out.
I push these thoughts away
and try to sing or hum
as I open the gate
and see Grandma
bending over
new pots of cuttings.

I am amazed at Grandma's
energy; even though she
is frail, she is determined.

She straightens up slowly
when she sees me.
'Ah, Sharnie dear,
thought you'd be coming
to see me soon.'
I reach to kiss her
and ask,
'How did you know?'
She taps her wrist,
'In my old broken bones,
I can feel things.'
I laugh. My grandma
says the funniest things
sometimes.
'When did you break
a bone, Grandma?' I ask.
'Oh, when I first married
Grandpa I helped chase
the cattle, fell over a rabbit hole
and broke my wrist.
So the good side of that
is it sends me twinges
every now and then.'
I look to see if Grandma
is joking, but she's not.

'Come,' and she takes me
to the back porch
where two teacups,
a steaming teapot
and a little plate
of homemade slice
sit waiting.

I put my notebook down
on the spare chair.
Grandma notices it,
so I say, 'We're doing
a project at school
on the Vietnam War.'

'A war project,' repeats Grandma,
the teapot wobbling
as she pours the tea
into delicate china teacups.
'Whatever for?' she mumbles.

'Well I thought you might
tell me a bit about Grandpa's
war, how it's different
to this war right now.'

Grandma pauses
and passes me the plate
of slice.
'Well in Grandpa's war

everyone used their
skills at home
to help the men on the front.
There were shortages of food
and clothing with all the men
serving overseas, and lots of
equipment and raw materials
used for the war effort,
so we'd knit –
why even the boys knitted
for the war effort.
We had ration cards,
we learned
to make do and craft,
grow lots of our own food.
Well everyone gardened then
and I always found
it soothing to watch seeds
or slips of green grow.
But using chemical warfare
is another thing.'

'What do you mean?' I ask,
brushing crumbs away
from my notebook,
as I write down points.
'Spraying the crops
and jungle with Agent Orange,
that's not right,' says Grandma,
and her hand shakes

so violently
that little drops of tea
fall on the dainty
embroidered cloth
like little drops of blood.

I feel sick and refuse
a second piece of slice.
'Rules of war have changed,'
sighs Grandma,
'not that there were
any sensible rules anyway,
but spraying chemicals,
killing and poisoning the soil
no matter if it's crops
or people in the way,
is another thing.'

We both grow quiet
and hear the blue wrens
making tiny noises in the bushes,
the wind chimes tinkle.
Will the moon get poisoned
by us too? I wonder.

Grandma sighs again,
then reaches for my hand.
'But I have my grandchildren
to love,' she says,
'treasure indeed.

Let me show you the cards
and postcards Grandpa
sent back to me
from overseas.'

I leave my notebook
next to my teacup
and for the next half-hour
Grandma shows me
card after card
with my grandpa's
beautiful handwriting looping
over scenes of flowers
or old buildings
or even little drawings
of himself and a description
of the food they ate.
'Sometimes food from the
jungle around them,'
says Grandma, 'he fought
in New Guinea.'

As I go to collect my things,
Grandma says,
'But those protestors,
they shouldn't get violent
or throw stones or bottles,
otherwise they are just
causing a different sort
of war on home soil.'

Consequences

At school on Monday,
Mr Grear, our principal,
speaks at the assembly.

'There was an incident
over the Anzac Day
weekend,
with young protestors
demonstrating.
If anyone at this school
was in their ranks
it will be instant expulsion.'

Everyone has shocked faces.
I don't mean to,
but I look over
to where Cas
is standing.
She doesn't have her head down;
her friends are beside her.
They look straight
ahead, too.

Mr Grear continues,
'It's time we explained
a few facts about conscription
or national service.'

'You mean Nashos,'
someone calls from the back
of the assembly.
We are standing
on the bitumen area
large enough to hold rows
and rows of students lined up
in forms.
I think I recognise that voice,
but although Mr Grear
looks and looks
from the rostrum,
he doesn't pick anyone out.

'Yes, Nashos, if you like,
and those who mock
the scheme should
show some national pride,
a sense of pride
for their country and—'

But Mr Grear's
prosing
doesn't get far.
Gail steps out
from our form line
and straightens
her shoulders.
She is fumbling

with something,
it's a framed photo.

She holds it above
her head and says,
'Here's a Nasho
and now he's dead.
Do we honour him?
War stinks!
We should all be protesting,'
she shouts,
and runs for the school gate.

Ellie is in our form
line, sniggering
and whispering to Marg,
making sure we all hear,
'Gail is so dramatic,
always making a scene …'

Everyone talks,
everyone turns to the student
beside them, behind them,
then Mr Grear dismisses
the assembly.

I see Miss Parkes
hurrying in the direction
Gail took.

On the way to class,
Mia talks about Gail.
'She's so twisted,
I can't believe she
supports protests!
She comes to school
in a mess,
no lunch, she's not like
everyone else.'

I don't say anything,
I'm too confused.

Mia continues,
'Ellie said Gail's brother
died in Vietnam …'

I suck in a sharp,
painful breath
and see a little picture
in my mind of Gail,
huddled with her mother
and her sister, so sad,
at the Anzac Day ceremony.
Now I'm
seeing Gail a bit
more clearly.

I feel choked up,
don't have the words

to say how I'm feeling.
Instead, I ask,
'But how does Ellie know?'
I can picture
Ellie's sharp eyes
and sharp teeth as she smiles
and shoots out stinging words.
'She knows everything,'
explains Mia, adding,
'well, she thinks she does.'

My head is a jumble.
As I look at Mia
a little thought
pops into my head.
She doesn't understand,
she thinks Gail
is a bit weird,
like Ellie does.
No, not as bad
as Ellie but …

I think of how Grandma
is still so sad about Grandpa,
about a war cutting his life
short, so that my mother missed
her father and how I never had
a grandpa to get to know.
And I get a bit fired up,
'Why can't

people protest?'
I ask.
And suddenly I feel
a bit of admiration
for Cas.
Cas and Gail have
more in common
than I thought.

I don't expect Mia
to answer my question.
She doesn't know about Cas,
and I don't want her
to know either,
but I'm not done.
'Mia, what's wrong
with protesting the Vietnam
War? We're learning about
it for our project, don't
you feel a bit sad for Gail,
losing her brother?
It wasn't his choice to
go to war.'

I look at Mia and she suddenly
seems changed. Her eyes are
flashing with anger and she's
not like the Mia
I thought I knew.
Then I notice a little

homemade badge
on her school uniform,
near the collar.
I've seen a little badge
like that on Ellie's uniform,
on Marg's uniform.
'What's that?'
I peer at the badge.
'Oh, just something Ellie made
and thought I might
like to wear also.'

Then Mia says, 'Seeya,'
and is gone without
a backwards glance.
She catches up with Ellie
and Marg and they
huddle together.

After school I want
to tell Cas about Mia,
about Gail,
but Cas walks away
quickly with her friends
to the bus stop.

Strive and strife

I overhear an argument
as Cas helps Mum
in the kitchen.
Apparently
Mr Grear sent home
a letter to all parents
about the Anzac Day protests,
and Mum is suspicious.

'Why didn't you come
with Grandma and us
to the ceremony?
You know how much
it means to Grandma,
to me actually …'
Mum falters a bit here.

Cas doesn't answer.
I can hear the clink of crockery
as she stacks dried dishes.

'And what's this Mr Grear says
about protests? Were students
involved from your school, Cas?'

Silence.

'You must know …
unless …' But Mum doesn't finish,
she tries a different tack.
'I know there is a lot
going on in the news
and in the world right now,
but Cas you need to put
all your energy into
your studies.'

Well that breaks the silence
from Cas.

'Studies? What good
will A's in Maths
and French and Literature be
when our soldiers return
wounded and damaged?
No one
thinks them heroes
like Grandpa and Uncle Tom
in earlier wars.'

Cas is flinging the
tea towel around,
emphasising each word
with a swoosh
of linen.

Then Mum says
something that really
shows what she's
thinking, but also shows
that she doesn't know Cas lately:
'But that's nothing
to do with your career, Cas.
You have the brains
to go to university,
something I never had
the chance to do.
Forget about the war
and start thinking
of your studies.
It would be just
as big a waste
if you let your
chance go.'

'Forget about bombing
and napalm and deaths?
All for what?'
Cas storms out
of the kitchen,
slams the back door
and is gone.

Something has to be done

The next day
on the bus
going home,
I overhear Cas
and her friends
talking behind hands,
heads slightly bent
as they huddle
on the back seat.

'How can we fight
someone else's war?
Tyson's friend Liam
just had his number
called up, and now
he's off to Vietnam.
He has no choice.
Not fair!'

Then someone else whispers,
'Protest … there's an
anti-war march
coming up.
Had one in the city
last year,
we can do one here.'

'But I heard that
protestors were hurt,'
Cas says,
'they had police horses,
some people threw rocks
and glass bottles.'

'Yeah, I heard it was
at the American Embassy,
wasn't it?'
'We'll need to
make posters,
placards, things like:
Stop Conscription
or *End War* …
You're good at posters
aren't you, Cas?'

Then Cas says,
'We can't, can we?
I don't want anyone
to get hurt.'

'Come on, Cas,
what about the
young blokes
in Vietnam
and the innocent
children?'
Tyson says.

'But here in
this little town?'
Cas persists.

'Why not?
Conscripts come from here,
we have a cenotaph,
we can march to that
or march around it.
Make it bigger than
what we started on
Anzac Day.'

Cas looks up suddenly,
right at me,
and frowns.
The whispering
gets even softer,
backs more
turned against me,
against other
passengers.

My head is
aching with
the idea of war,
protest, police.

I feel a growing pain.
I am losing Cas,

the Cas I share
my bedroom with,
the Cas I share
my mum, my dad with,
the Cas I share
the walk to the
school bus with,
the Cas I share
the chores with.
She is growing up,
growing away
and I miss her.
She spends more
time with her friends,
with Tyson,
than me.
Lucky I can still
talk with Grandma.

Tears upon tears

I push open Grandma's gate
like I always do, I want
to talk, to tell her about Mia,
how she doesn't feel like
my friend anymore,
how Cas is planning
more protests,
about Tyson,
about Mum and Cas …
I just want someone
to listen,
really listen,
and Grandma does
that so well.

Even though I knock
a few times
the door is locked,
Grandma's door is
never locked.
She isn't on her back porch
or with her pots and plants.
I sigh and head back out
the gate and run to our house.
'Mum,' I call, trying
to stretch the sound

so it hollers into
every corner.

But there is no answer.

I find her
in the kitchen,
head down
on the table,
crying.
Really crying:
my mother with
red, swollen eyes.
She cries harder
when she sees me.

'Darling,' she manages,
'come here.'
She waits until
she has her arms
around my waist.
'Grandma has passed away,'
she sobs.

My world is spinning
and I hear a howl.
I know it's me,
a wild pain-filled howl
and I'm running,

running out of the house,
down the backyard,
finding a place to hide,
to curl, just me
and this deep
ache inside.

As I gulp for air, hiccup,
I think about Grandma,
then try to see tomorrow
and the day after, in a world
without her. But I can't.
My head and whole body
just hurt too much.

I see a figure
coming down
the backyard,
like a ghost wavering.
'Sharnie,' says the figure
softly, and I hear Cas's
voice wobbly with tears.

She puts her arms
around me
and we cry
a little more together.
I feel like a tea towel
twisted until
there is not a drop

of moisture left.
'Come inside,
Mum has made sandwiches.
We'll have hot tea
with sugar in it.'

I feel a stab of pain
as I remember
this was exactly
Grandma's remedy
for shock
or sadness, or if you hurt
yourself gardening,
like the time
I tried to help her
prune her thorny roses.

Mum is talking
on the phone again.
'It's Dad,' she mouths to us,
'he's coming home tomorrow.'
Cas lets go of me,
moves away and says,
'Great, that's all I need.'

A changed world

It's the May school holidays,
so I don't have to face school,
friends, a routine,
as if everything is normal.

The world feels
thick and sticky
like a spider's web.

After a while
my head aches.
'It's grief,' explains Mum.
Even Cas has red eyes
and her mascara runs in wild
black smudges on her cheeks.

Neighbours come,
relatives come,
uncles, aunts,
and Lewis seems
to stay at our place
all the time.
The sparkle has gone
from his eyes,
he mopes around,
follows me just like
Jules my cat.

I decide I have to
change all that,
try to make him
think of something
else, other than
Grandma.

I show him the day's headlines
from the newspaper,
we read about the preparation
for the moon landing,
how Commander Armstrong
will be the first out
of the Lunar Module
to stand on the moon.
'That's because he's nearest
the exit,' says Lewis,
like it's the most obvious
bit of information around.

Later that evening
as night falls
we look up at the sky.
We are tracking the moon,
and Lewis says:
'Maybe Grandma will get
a great view of the moon
landing from heaven.'
If I wasn't so sad
I would laugh

at Lewis, instead
I watch as a globule
of spider thread unwinds
like a fissure
of moon parachuting down.
The spider thread
is as white as
moonlight floating,
sticky floating,
trying to entangle
on anything it passes,
maybe a branch,
a fence, a blade of grass.

I hold out my hand
to catch it
and maybe catch
a message,
a connection.

Floating cobwebs
mean rain coming,
well that's what
Grandma used to say,
and I feel her so close
in this huge vast sky.
I sigh, and Lewis nestles
close, and we stare
at the moon

and think of Grandma
holding us,
cuddling us.

How can peace cause arguments?

Dad comes home,
takes charge,
notices things
that Mum hasn't.
She's been so busy
with Grandma.

When Dad tidies up
the lounge room,
he notices the *Peace* badge
Cas has stuck to her schoolbag,
but does he know about Tyson?

Dad asks Cas a question.
'I've heard about a group
of protestors at the school.
They disrupted
the Anzac Day service.
Mum also told
me about them,
and I've read the principal's
letter. You're not one
of them, are you, Cas?
We're concerned
you're mixing
with the wrong crowd.'

Cas's face goes from
red to paper white,
but she stays
quiet.

'And this,'
Dad hasn't finished yet –
he pulls a poster
from an envelope
he's holding.
'I found this in the mail
addressed to you, Cas.
What's going on?'

It's a poster,
the same one I've glimpsed
being passed among
Cas's friends
on the school bus.
There's a soldier – maybe
American or Australian –
barbed wire
and a crying baby.
I hate it. And I screw
up my eyes tightly.

Dad whips around to me.
'Looks like you've seen
this before, Sharnie.
Where?'

I gasp and look
at Cas and then
back at Dad
and Mum,
wiping away more tears.
I want to cry, too.
Secrets, loyalty.
To who?
Mum? Dad? Cas?
'Um,' I begin.
But Cas butts in.
'She doesn't know
anything
about the poster.
Or about the Vietnam War
or the protest.
She's too young.'

I'm shocked.
Cas is protecting me
and at the same time
telling me
I'm still a baby.
A wild thought
runs through my head.
I could prove
I wasn't a baby,
by blabbing about
the Anzac Day protest,
about Cas knowing Tyson.

Then I think
of the red pompom
on Cas's beanie
bobbing along among
a sea of banners
and hear Grandma's
words again
about Cas.
I stay silent.

Dad waits for me
to say something.
I can see he looks sad
and disappointed.
I don't feel good
but I've made a choice.
I should be glad about that.

Dad turns back to Cas.
'I'll not have rubbish like that
in our house, Cas.
Not ever.
Nor will I have a daughter
of mine disgracing us
by protesting the laws
of our nation.
Understood?
I don't want to monitor
your mail
so you need to make

sure no more
posters like this
come to our house.'

He tears the envelope
and poster to shreds
and leaves
the scraps
on the floor.

Patriotism

A few days later
Mum suggests
a visit to Grandma's house
and Lewis is going to come, too.

Not Cas, she gets ready
to go out. 'Meet my friends,'
she says when Dad asks
where she is going to.

'Your friends,' Dad repeats.
'Surely not the friends who are
leading you astray,
the protesting, poster-sending
friends?'
Cas's eyes blaze, but again
she holds her tongue.
Dad is getting revved up now.
'Your friends,' he says again,
'are no better than Communists.
Enemies. Your grandfather,
your uncle, fought
for a better Australia
and now we have
to protect it again.
The war is nearly
on our doorstep.

All the farming families
and little regional towns
I visit with my job,
are all afraid
of a close neighbouring
country becoming
Communist run.'

Cas hoists her bag
onto her shoulder
and reaches for
the back door handle.

'Cas!' Dad's voice is loud now.
'Have some respect
for your mother,
your grandmother,
can't you help
in the garden today?'

But Cas has yanked
open the door
and is walking quickly
down the path.

Dad sort of crumples a bit,
gives a watery smile to Mum,
and says to Lewis, 'How's the moon
landing countdown going?'

Dad doesn't wait for a reply;
he goes outside too, but
heads for the chook pens.

A garden without a gardener

Mum, Lewis and I walk
in silence to Grandma's house.

I am crying softly
when I know for sure
Grandma isn't there.
Mum says,
'You two will know
what flowers we can pick
for Grandma's funeral.
What she liked best.'

We nod and walk
to the back porch
where Grandma
kept her secateurs,
her string, her little packet
of gathered seeds,
shells, pots, feathers,
broken pottery.
And it's then that I see
the head of the red horse,
resting on a white quartz rock,
nestled under a piece
of Grandma's special
speckled geranium.

She has left me treasure.
I must have missed this
when I swept up the broken
pieces.
It doesn't need to say,
For you, Sharnie.

Before Mum leaves
I say, 'I know Grandma
kept forgetting things,
but she was good
at remembering about
us and her garden …'
I can't quite put
the words together.

'Ah, Sharnie,
your grandmother
was getting very frail, too.'

We gather roses,
lavender spikes,
bottlebrush stems,
rosemary,
geraniums, lilies
and some
sheaths of fern greenery.
We fill buckets
with them.

'And this, too,' says Lewis,
as he plucks
a long plume
from among
a bunch of feathers.
It is red and green
and we recognise
it from the parrots
that come to feed
in Grandma's garden.

Mum comes over to help
carry the flowers home.
'Will you arrange
the flowers, Sharnie?
For the church?
I'll go back later
and unlock Grandma's house
and get down her
big crystal vases.'

I slowly nod my head.
I feel a tiny warmth
of happiness,
I can do this
for Grandma;
it would be what
she wanted.

Dad is getting the lawn
mower out ready
for our lawns.
'I will do Grandma's
lawns, too,'
he says to Mum.

I feel teary again,
remembering Grandma
and her old
hand-pushed mower.
I should have helped
mow her lawns.

Is this what it really
feels like
to lose someone?
Remembering all the things
you should have
done for them?

Who can I tell
all my worries
and secrets to
now Grandma is gone?

Saying goodbye

I focus on my vases
of flowers as hard
as I can while
the funeral service
unfolds.
Dad reads out a timeline
of Grandma's life,
(I listened when Dad sat
at the kitchen table
and asked Mum
and Aunty Jessy
questions about
Grandma's life.)
Mum is too upset
to stand at the front
and read.
Dad even recounts
a little funny story
to share, but it's
when the coffin
is lifted onto Dad's
and some other men's
shoulders,
that I just cry and cry.

Mum and my aunt
file down after the coffin,

arms around each other,
then it's Cas
and me and Lewis.
Our neighbour
pushes Uncle Tom
in a wheelchair.
I just concentrate
on the outline
of Mum's figure
because I am
crying so much,
I can't see where
I am going,
or even any of the other
people in the pews
standing either side
waiting for the family
to leave the church first.

At home, I help Mum pile
plates with sandwiches,
scones, slices
and pass around
cups of tea, but it is so
full of people wanting
to hug and ask questions,
or use our bedroom
to put their cardigans in
and powder their cheeks
after crying,

that I go again
to Grandma's garden.

I just want to sit at Grandma's
table on the porch,
look at her flowers
smell their fragrance
and think of Grandma
by myself.

JULY 1969

Not me, not me

Once a year,
there are form photos.
Cas has warned me
about these:
'Take a comb
to tidy your hair,
and a tissue
to polish your shoes
beforehand.'
Really?
I look at Cas when
she tells me this
and I see she's
not joking.
Serious.

After lunch each class
is directed to
the library
for their photos.
The photographer
gives directions:
'Right hand over
left please …
and wear your smiles.
Ready?'
Click! Click!

I feel
as if I've changed into
a different person
to the one who
was in the class
before the holidays.

Mia is trying hard
to get me to smile,
even poking me in the ribs.
I know this class photo
will be a bit of history
in the making, just like
the photo Grandma
showed me of Grandpa
with his army regiment,
but that thought makes
me sad. Until I think
of one of Grandpa's funny
postcards of a drawing
of him cooking
in the New Guinea jungle.
And I smile. But the smile
vanishes when I see Mia
nudging Ellie and they are
both smirking into cupped
hands and looking at Gail's
back. *KICK ME* is written
in capital letters in red biro.

I reach past everyone
scrambling to move away
from crossed legs and hands,
and pull the note from
Gail's shirt.

Gail swings around,
an accusing look
on her face.
She sees the note
and glares at me.
'Did you do
that, Sharnie?'
'No!' I protest
and look towards
Mia and Ellie.
Ellie makes
a kicking motion
with her foot.
Ellie's friend Marg
leans into her
and they both laugh
and walk away.
Mia looks at me once,
tosses her head
and follows quickly,
locks her arm into
Marg's and they
waltz away.

'Oh!' mumbles Gail.
'Thanks.'
And she walks off
shoulders hunched.
I am left standing
by myself. My whole
world has tilted.

More, yet more revelations

After the class photos,
lessons resume
and it's Geography –
the Vietnam War
project.

Miss Parkes fires
the first question.
'Let's discuss this current war,'
she begins. 'What words come
to mind?'
'Conscription,' Marg shouts.

'What is it?' Miss Parkes asks,
as she writes the word
conscription
on the chalkboard.

Gail answers,
'It's forcing boys to go
to war, when they didn't
volunteer.'

'No!' shouts Ellie.
'It's a way of defending
our country
from another country.'

'Like who?' demands Gail.
It's as if there is only
her and Ellie in the class
and they want to fight
with words.
'A Communist country,'
answers Ellie. 'Communists
will overrun our country
if we aren't careful.'

'I can't see anyone
overrunning our country,'
shouts Gail,
'but I can see our soldiers
fighting and dying
in another country.
And some soldiers didn't
volunteer to fight,
they were forced.'

Everyone is talking
at once.
Miss Parkes is
waving her hands
for quiet, then the bell goes
and no one waits
for Miss Parkes
to officially send us out.

Miss Parkes is yelling
above all our noise,
'We'll have this
discussion
again, girls.
Think about it.'
Everyone
scrambles
and jostles
and shouts.

Rifts, so wide

A few days later in class,
Mia passes me a newspaper
clipping
stuck between
a science textbook.
I twirl a hank of hair
between my fingers,
pretending I'm studying
a diagram on the food chain,
when really I look
at the photo
of a protestor wearing
a sandwich board.
We don't want to kill, it says.
I nod my head;
I don't want to either.

But it's when I unfold
the cutting further
and read what Mia
has written
that I get a reality check.
Sharnie and Gail,
make a ridiculous filling
for this sandwich.

Was it only a few weeks ago
Mia and I giggled
through class?
Now every little bit
of laughing magic has gone,
abracadabra, vanishimo,
and thinking about that
makes me cry.
A few tears wet
the newspaper cutting.
Mia snatches it back,
glares at me
and slides into
the vacant spot
at Ellie's desk.

Preparing for our own moon landing

Miss Parkes has splashed
the words *Apollo 11*
across the chalkboard.

'You know the Kennedy Space Centre
has had a dress rehearsal
for the moon landing, so
now we are going to design
our own moon landing poster,
putting our own imaginative spin
on this major event.'

Everyone is chattering, squealing.
Usually our Geography lessons
are pretty predictable
and sometimes very boring.
But posters? In Geography?

'Groups of three,'
says Miss Parkes.
'You'll have
a chance to decide
what the moon landing
will look like,
or even what
you think will

be discovered
on the moon.
Mr Grear wants
the long corridor
decorated in space theme.

'I'll read to you
what is suggested here:
This is the event
of the twentieth century.
The moon is finally
to be reached by man
and our school
will have a celebration
to showcase
our students' flair in Art,
Science, Geography
and future thinking.
By the way, the local
press will be here
after the event
to take photos
and interview students.
There will be a prize
for Best Group Effort.'

A huge buzzing noise
hums as everyone shares
excited comments

and suggestions
with their friends.

I look over to where Mia
is jumping on the spot
and laughing with Marg
and Ellie.

'So …' begins Miss Parkes
again in a loud voice,
'we need you to
form groups. I hope
you can do this quietly
and sensibly.'

Everyone is calling,
grabbing a friend
to huddle in a group.
I look and see Gail
is just standing there.
'Gail, want to join me?'

Gail looks over,
notices that I am alone
and slowly nods.
It seems a reluctant
nod, but neither of us
has a choice,
we are the odd
ones out.

We look a bit
awkwardly
at each other,
unsure of what to do.
Then Miss Parkes
booms out another
suggestion.
'Sheets of paper are
at the front of the room.'

I go and take
several sheets for Gail
and me.
'Any ideas?' I ask Gail,
but she's silent.
I wonder about Cas,
and her poster making.
What would she draw?
She would use huge
lettering maybe,
and an image.
Then I say,
'Craters on the moon,
but no cows jumping
over the moon
in the craters.'
I don't know why I say
this, maybe because
I'm finally realising
that Mia will never

laugh with me again
about nursery rhymes
and moon jingles.

This seems to do
the trick for Gail;
she quickly sketches
an astronaut
peering into a crater
and finding
a pile of love notes
all about moonbeams
with silver and blood-red
hearts.

I'm surprised
I can still laugh
and Gail joins in.
'That's very clever, Gail,'
I say.

Miss Parkes comes
over to see what
we're laughing about
and then brings the class
to attention.
'If you're looking
for a starting point,
try something

a bit out of the ordinary
like Gail has done here.'

And without asking Gail,
Miss Parkes
whisks the sketch up
and shows the class.
'Great,' someone says.
'Funny,' says someone else.
'A bit over the top,'
comes another comment,
and I see Ellie smirking
and bumping Mia
with her elbow.

I glance at Gail
to see her reaction,
but she just shrugs
and begins another sketch
on the next sheet.
This time it's a big moon
and a tiny Earth,
with an astronaut saying,
*'I can still see the Vietnam War
from outer space.'*
And I think that's the sort
of poster Cas needs to make,
but aloud I say, 'Gosh, Gail,
that packs a punch.'

'Isn't that what a
poster should do?'
she says, and quickly
screws up the sheet.

'I hate war,' she adds
quietly, sadly.
'What about you, Sharnie?'
she asks after a while.

I pause and try to think
of the words to show
how jumbled my
life has become.
'My grandpa died in the last war
and I know how much
my grandma missed him
and Cas is protesting
this war, I guess I'm still
figuring things out …'
It sounds a bit lame,
but Gail accepts
it and says,
'I have to leave school
in another year or so,
get a job in a shop,
get any sort of job really.
Mum is by herself
and doesn't earn much.
Besides, when she was

called to the principal's office
after I walked out,
he suggested it would
be best if I left school
and got a job.'

'What?' I try to keep
my voice down.
'What right has he
got to dictate your life?
With your imagination
and your hands, you could
draw anything.'

Miss Parkes interrupts us
and returns the first sketch.
'Of course,' she adds, 'groups
can show more factual things
like some science knowledge
of the space landing, or some
geography of the moon itself.'

'Sounds like too much
hard work,' mutters Gail.

'How about aliens from
outer space like my cousin
Lewis thinks are flying
around somewhere?'
I suggest.

Gail's pencil
sketches quickly.
I laugh as green
frog-shaped aliens
with long antennas
like television receptors
appear marching towards
the *Apollo 11* spaceship
resting on the moon.

'Wow! We will have
the best poster
for sure!
We might have a chance
of winning because
you are the
best artist here,'
I say to Gail.

I admire the magic
that flows from her
like the night sky
aglow with a trail
of tiny twinkling stars.
Like the magic Grandma
created with flowers
and plants, a green
kaleidoscope of colours
humming with insects.

'How about we work
on this idea more
and maybe
we can colour in
or do collage with pages
from one of the weekly
magazines?' suggests Gail.

I nod and think sadly
that Mia would have loved
collage. I can feel
Ellie looking over
and I stare back.
Ellie makes a heart shape
with her hands,
then a smashing motion.
Mia mimics her and I feel
a surge of anger,
we need to win this competition.

Ellie's group,
which includes
Marg and Mia,
are designing
the lunar shuttle
complete with
a self-serve cafeteria.
I know this because
it was the next poster

after ours that Miss Parkes
showed the class
to spur
us on.

I really feel I could do
this, win with Gail,
win for Grandma, for Cas,
for Gail, for me.

Mail-order aliens

My feet naturally walk
towards Grandma's house
after school and I find
Lewis there, just sitting
on the back step.

He looks up at me
as I claim a spot next to him.
'I wish Grandma
was still here,' he says.

I give Lewis a hug
and we sit for a while.

Then, just like Lewis,
he pulls a comic book
from his schoolbag
and shows me
the back page
where he's circled
a mail-order coupon
for space guns.

'I've nearly saved for
this one,' and he skewers
the picture of a big gun

with his finger.
It looks like a bug catcher,
not like a gun at all.
And bugs might be
all it will catch,
but I don't tell
Lewis that.

'Do you think you'll
need protection
from outer space?'
'Sure,' he replies, then adds,
'or from those protestors.'
'Protestors?
You mean the ones
we saw on Anzac Day?'
I'm really listening
to Lewis now.
And surprised also
that he can remember.

'Yeah, saw them again
walking with Cas,
one laughed at
my moon boots.
Cas said to him,
"He's only a kid, Tyson."
Tyson said I should
have my feet planted

firmly on earth,
whatever that means.'

'But how do you know
they were the same people
at the Anzac Day march?' I ask.

'Because
they were talking about it
as I came up to them.
Something about Cas
making posters this time.
Thought Cas would
like to see
my moon boots.'

I just stare at Lewis
trying to take in all
this information,
but he's pushed himself
up now and is holding
the comic in one hand,
his schoolbag
in the other.

'Gotta go,' he says.
'Would have liked to tell
Grandma about my space gun,
but you're like her, Sharnie.'

And Lewis surprises me again
as he bumps his forehead
against mine. 'A space kiss,'
he says and heads for his house.

I'm staring after Lewis,
wanting to both laugh
and cry
in equal measure.
Grandma, I think,
is this how
grief feels?
Sad, lonely
and almost like an alien
encounter at the same time?

As I walk slowly home
I see the soft milky blush
of the moon in
the afternoon sky
and ask, 'Moon,
why do we have war?
Why?'

Hungry for new friendship

Gail and I are walking
down the wide school corridor
at lunchbreak.
This morning I waited
till her bus arrived,
then we both went to class.
Since designing
the poster together
all I've wanted
is to talk to Gail
before class,
in class,
at lunchtime.
Mia filled those gaps
for me,
but not anymore.
I can't believe
how much
I want to chat
about the weekend
or the countdown
to the *Apollo 11* launch,
anything really,
just to chat.
It's not long now
until the moon landing,
and I want to share

the excitement with
someone.
I just begin to ask
Gail about our poster,
when Ellie and Marg
deliberately
veer over
and bump into Gail.
I move out of the way
but Gail stands her
ground.
That annoys
Ellie even more.
'Can't feel anything
can you?'
Then she chants,
'All hail to Gail
the fail-ure.'

Heads turn;
one of Cas's friends
says to Ellie,
'That's enough.'
Ellie actually flushes red
and pulls Marg away
around the corner.

I look at Gail.
'Sorry,' I say.
'Nothing to be sorry for,'

she answers,
'that's just Ellie.
Her brother was friends
with my big brother
before he died.'
Then Gail says
her brother's name
like she's saying
a foreign word,
a hard-to-pronounce word:
'Steve.'
I look at Gail
with new knowledge,
slowly, oh so slowly,
finding out who she is,
through her brother,
through her family.

'Gail,' I begin, 'my grandma
died before the school holidays,
I—'
But I can't say any more
and stumble back
to my locker through a mist
of tears. I grab a fresh hanky
out and my lunch bag.

Gail holds the door of
my locker open.
'I'm sorry about your

grandma,' she says.
'It really hurts
deep inside, doesn't it?'
I nod, blow my nose
and close and lock the door.

Outside on the hill
we find a grassy spot
to sit.

Gail has no lunch
so I twist and break
my apple and share
my sandwich.
'Thank you,' says Gail.
'I'll pay you back
one day.'

Then she turns away
and bites into the sandwich
as if she needs energy
to say words that
won't come out.

I don't know what
to say either
so I eat my apple.
Neither of us mentions
the words, *death* or
killed or *grief.*

Sometimes just being
with a friend without
having to use words
is special.
A crumb gets caught
in my throat,
makes me cough
and splutter
as I realise
what I've thought:
Gail is a friend,
my friend.

Does Gail have a grandma?
I must find out.
I now know
she had a brother
called Steve,
and she has
a little sister.
But why doesn't
she have lunch?
I'm not sure
I can ask her
that yet.

Instead, I talk
about the full moon
watery and chalky
in the sky above us,

and think of our poster
waiting to be collaged.
I have an idea:
'Gail, I was wondering
if you want to come
over to my place?
We can work on the poster,
get a headstart and really
make it shine for
the competition?'

I'm surprised my words
come out smoothly;
I don't usually jump
at an idea before
thinking it through.

Gail swallows the last
of her apple and smiles.
'I'd like that, Sharnie.'

From Cas with …

As we go back to class,
Cas is looking in her locker,
pushing folders aside
and trying
to stop her textbooks
from toppling out.
Gail deftly catches some
but a poster rolls out
and I look in horror
at a corner with black
letters dripping red.
Gail looks at Cas
quickly and nods,
but Cas is jittery
and tries to stuff
everything back
in the locker.
'Maybe I can help
you stack it in properly
so this can be
hidden better?'

As Gail says this
we see Mr Grear walking
down the corridor,
a word here,
a spot check there.

Cas glares at me
but accepts Gail's offer
and they begin the neat
reorganisation,
with the poster first
on the floor of the locker.

'Ah,' says Mr Grear as he
stops near us. 'Just
wanted to express
my condolences
on the loss of
your grandmother,
Cas, Sharnie.
She was an early
member of the
School Mothers' Club.'
He pauses and looks
at Cas's locker.
'You'll all be running
late for class, no time
for a spring clean now.'
Then he is on his way
again.

'Phew!' Cas is shaking.
'Thanks Gail.' And
she nods slightly
at me. Then I pull

Gail away
and we head
for our classroom.

Eavesdropping

Later, before teatime,
Cas is talking on the phone.
She wraps the cord
around her wrist
and tucks her legs
under the small
telephone chair.
Her fluffy slippers
jiggle as she swings
her feet backwards
and forwards.

'Really?' she says sweetly
as if her mouth is full
of coconut rough chocolate,
her favourite.
Then her words become
a bit more breathy
as if she's having trouble
hearing, thinking, speaking.
'Is that a good idea?'
she whispers.
'But that's when
the school celebration
will be held … Reporters? …
Yes, I can see that the protest
would be …'

Cas notices me staring
and waves me away.
One of her
slippers falls off.

'Hold on for a mo,'
she interrupts
the person on
the other end
of the line.
She cups
her hand over
the mouthpiece
and says
in a snooty voice,
'This is a private conversation.
Don't you have homework
to do? Shoo!'

I take the hint and
walk towards the back door.
As I leave, I hear Cas laugh
to the other person
and say, 'No, not a cat
just my little sister!'

Messages delayed, delayed

Lewis comes charging into
the backyard. I'm just
thinking, dreaming
and running
my hands along
Jules's back.

Jules jumps up
with a long flick
of her tail and
takes off.

Lewis is a flash
of silver;
wrinkled,
breaking-apart silver.
'Message from the moon,'
he drones.

His hair is sticking out
and his thin
arms look like
they need
a feed of Grandma's
chocolate slice.
Ah, that thought shoots
a pain into my chest.

But I've thought up other
space questions for Lewis,
that might make him smile.

'Which has the least gravity:
Earth or the moon?'

'Oh, easy peasy,' says Lewis.
'The moon, of course! That's
why the astronauts will
wear heavy oxygen packs
when they walk
on the moon.'

'Hmm,' I sigh.
'Now, is that message
really from the moon?'

'Nah, just kidding,
it's from Grandma.'

'What?' I'm stunned.
I look confused,
feel confused.
'But … Grandma's dead,'
I say. Perhaps Lewis
has forgotten that
or maybe
he has strange powers …

my mind
is in turmoil.

Lewis fishes around in his
pocket and pulls out a note,
then fluff, watermelon seeds
and lolly wrappers also.

'Sorry,' he whispers, and he looks
like the little boy he really is.
His space boots are peeling
apart and his hands are
covered in layers of dirt.
'Lewis,' I begin, but he
hasn't finished.

'I was folding
paper into spaceships,
planes. Grandma gave
it to me the day
before she died.'
Then Lewis suddenly
throws a folded plane
at me
made of Grandma's note.
He zooms away,
arms outstretched,
silver moulting
like a bird.
Maybe too much

space exposure,
I think.

I unfold the paper plane;
my hands shake
at every crease.

Can you visit me
this weekend, Sharnie?
I have something for you.
Love and kisses, Grandma.

This time Grandma's writing
is not all hieroglyphics,
just the last line is in symbols,
crosses and noughts
for kisses and cuddles.
I feel a sharp longing
to know what Grandma
wanted to give me.
I clutch the note like
it's the greatest treasure
and sigh.

'Oh, Grandma.' I dissolve
into tears and think about
her in her own little pyramid,
safely at rest, the artefacts
of her life growing
in profusion around her.

We are history in the making

Mia grabs me from behind
and swings me
and my big schoolbag
around in a circle.
I spiral into Ellie and Marg
and both Ellie and I sprawl
across the corridor floor.

'Idiot,' she snarls.
'And look at your hair,
Sharnie, wild like
a cat licked it clean.'

I'm sort of winded
and can't reply.
Gail is holding
her hand out to me,
then holds her hand
out to Ellie.
'I can get up myself.
Out of the way!'

Ellie grabs Marg
and they storm off.
Mia turns back to me,
sneers then
follows Ellie and Marg.

I am breathless.
How can Mia have
changed so much?
I have to stop myself
from crying; I can't keep
crying every time
something happens.

'Don't worry about them,'
whispers Gail, 'they're
just jealous.'

'Really?' I smile a watery
smile and wonder
how jealousy can turn
to spite.

We walk quietly
to our first class.

'Concentrate please.
You all need
to hand in your answers
to the Geography assignment
first thing tomorrow morning,'
says Miss Parkes.

No one is listening,
we are fidgety
and talkative.

‘Okay,’ she finally booms,
‘let’s go through some
of the questions now.
Ellie, what do you think
about organised protests
as a solution to social unrest?’

I want to laugh
at the stunned look
on Ellie’s face.
‘Um …’ she begins. ‘I …’

‘Alright, Gail, your
opinion please.
Ellie is more concerned
about whispering
and passing on messages,
which itself could be called
a social issue.’

Gail doesn’t hesitate.
‘This is supposed to be
a democratic country.
If people see the need
to protest
then they should.’

Marg interrupts,
‘But not with violence
or sit-ins.’

'Good point,' encourages
Miss Parkes.

'But,' says Gail,
'if you look back
at other events,
like women's right
to vote,
they had to chain
themselves to fences
to get their point
across.'

'That was past history,'
hisses Ellie.

'Yes, but they changed
laws in this country
because of it!'
Gail is hissing
now too.

'Ah!' Miss Parkes
is triumphant.
'So you've answered
one of the questions
for the assignment:
that protest movements
can change our
lawmakers' minds.'

‘Communists,’ mutters Ellie
in a small voice.
‘That’s what my dad
reckons if we don’t
support the Vietnam War.’

‘Is he going to support it
by going in the army
himself?’ shouts Gail.
‘Or will he let your
brother go instead?’

Ellie storms across to Gail’s
desk and yanks Gail’s long
ponytail.

I jump up and try to pull
them apart.
‘Stop it!’ I scream at Ellie.
I’m still bruised from
the fall earlier and I’m
just as angry as Ellie and Gail.

Miss Parkes
has social turmoil
happening here in her class.

Mr Grear is called in
and the class dismissed.

Gail and Ellie remain
with the two teachers.

During the next lesson
Gail comes back and sits
next to me.
'What happened?'

'I have detention after school,'
she says, 'and Mum has been
called in to see the principal.'

'What about Ellie?' I ask.
'Same fate as me.'

I put an arm
around Gail's shoulder.
I think fleetingly that a
few months ago,
I would have thought
putting an arm around
Gail's shoulder almost
as impossible as man
walking on the surface
of an out-of-reach moon.

Later, as we head
to the bus queues
I say to Gail,

'We could do something
at the school showcase –
an open letter of protest
for everyone to sign?'

Gail nods absently
and I remember Cas's
phone conversation.
Maybe there is already
a protest being organised?

Love is still an explosion

Cas is walking home with me
today. I know she wants
to tell me something.
It's like her words have gone
rusty from lack of practice.
'You know Dad is taking
a new job, helping our
neighbour Ted with
his building business?'
She waits for my reaction.
'Great, so he will be home
all the time now,' I reply.

Cas nods, 'But there's a catch.
He might find out more about
the protest movement,
and Tyson.'

I nod, secretly thrilled
that at last
Cas is confiding in me.
But it's a warning
she's throwing at me:
'So don't say anything,
anything
that might
cause trouble.'

We've stopped walking
and Cas is facing me,
searching my face.
'Of course, Cas.
I can keep your secrets.'
She sort of *humphs*
and powers on ahead.

A few minutes later
when we arrive home,
it's like Cas's predictions
have come true.
Dad is waiting by
the back door,
a grim look on his face
and Mum is holding a letter.
It shakes wildly
like a captured butterfly
in her hand.

My stomach does a crazy flip.
It's one of Cas's love letters
from Tyson.

'You've got a boyfriend?
Didn't we agree
to wait until you'd
finished high school
before you thought

of a boyfriend?'
Mum explodes.

'And this Tyson sounds
way too old for you, Cas.
Is he the reason you're
tangled up in this protest
movement? Is this how
you got those posters?
What's going on, Cas?
We are your parents,
we need to know,
to protect you.'

Dad speaks then,
'Cas, you are so bright,
so clever, can't you see
for yourself that this Tyson
is leading you astray,
leading you away
from what we believe in?
What is right for Australia!
And why all the secrecy?'

Cas fires up.
'Is it right that young men
are forced to fight a war
that will change their whole
future, where they might

have to kill or be killed?
The world is changing, Dad,
we're about to see
man land on the moon!
There's no time for
old-fashioned ideas, can't you
see that?' Cas is shouting,
trying to emphasise
what she's saying,
as if Dad and Mum's
only problem
is their deafness
to her words.

'Love doesn't wait,'
adds Cas as if she's
repeating words
from a song.
But then she throws
in another line:
'Death doesn't wait either.'

Mum sinks into a chair
and sobs, really sobs.
Cas stands by helpless,
tears silently running
down her face, too.
Dad sits down next to Mum
and holds her close.

I think, *Grandma,*
she's sobbing for you.
And maybe for Cas,
the old lost Cas.

New ways for new times

Cas is sitting in front
of the dressing table,
staring absently
picking up her hairbrush,
then clips, then ribbons,
then dropping them back down.

'Cas,' I say gently,
'you know Gail,
well she's coming to visit,
this weekend.'
I plough on hurriedly,
'We are doing posters for the
space landing competition …
We want to work on them here.'

I wait for Cas's reaction
to the word 'poster'.
It is no longer
an ordinary word.
'Hmm,' is all Cas says,
so I continue,
'We want to win
this competition and make
a protest of sorts.'

Cas turns to me now.
'Protest' is another word
that's changed.
'You, Sharnie? Do you even
know what's going on?
Mum and Dad won't be happy.'

'But I won't tell them
until we do our little protest.
We can't not do anything.
You know about Gail's brother?'
Cas nods slowly.
'Well, we've been doing
a Vietnam War project
for school and I'm learning
heaps. I'm not a baby
anymore,' and these last words
come out with a shout.

'Okay, okay, I can see you're
growing up, Sharnie, and it
would be good to have
someone in this family
on my side. But,' she warns,
'don't make too much
of a mess.'
And I know Cas means
our bedroom, not a mess
of protesting.

Cas loves our bedroom,
our little world, her little
world, ordered and private.
Where she can listen to
the radio, write notes
to Tyson, and dream
and cry.

Then I remember about
the bus conversation and
Tyson asking Cas to make
posters.
'Are you making posters, too?'
I ask.

'Maybe,' is all Cas will say.

In anticipation

On Friday afternoon
we wait for the buses.
Gail waves to me
across the mass
of students.
'See you tomorrow,'
she mouths.
Mia turns
in the next bus line
and I see the longing
on her face,
just for a moment
as she steps up
onto a bus
for the outskirts
of town.

I wave back to Gail
and I feel both excited
and nervous.
How will we talk
and act out of
the school environment?
Will she like our place?
Jules the cat?
Will we get the posters
done and could we

win the competition?
What will Cas think
of Gail and the poster?
What will Dad think?
But this *is* for school,
a project …

Collage is like life

I help Cas do our Saturday
morning jobs, like
banging the big bedroom
rug on the rail of the
outside stair and reluctantly
tidying my half of the room,
while Cas dusts and polishes
the dressing table and mirror.

Gail's mother drops her off
at our house and we are
a bit lost for words at first,
then Jules comes to the
front lawn to investigate
and Gail is won over
immediately. 'What a cat,'
she croons. 'You never
said you had a cat, Sharnie.'

We let Jules roll over and play
with a little ball of string.
Then I say, 'Want to meet
the rest of my family?'
Gail trails behind me
into the kitchen where Mum
is baking biscuits and Dad
is having his never-ending

cup of coffee.
'Hi,' says Gail. Dad says,
'Good to meet a new friend
of Sharnie's.'
And Mum offers us biscuits.

Then we talk for a bit
and I say, 'We'd better
get started on our Geography project.'
Dad asks, 'What is it, Sharnie?'
I feel a bit short of breath,
but Gail speaks up, 'I've
brought *Women's Weeklys* to
cut up for our collage. It's sort
of art, sort of science, for the
moon landing competition.'

Dad nods,
Mum sends me a
searching look,
then I lead the way
to my bedroom.

'Hi Cas,' says Gail.
'Hi,' replies Cas as we
spread our magazines,
pens, scissors over
the very clean rug.
As we unfold our posters
Cas peers over my shoulder.

Gail seizes an opportunity.
'Which one, Cas, should we
enter for the competition –
the crater and love notes
or green frog aliens?'

I wait, not looking at Cas.
It's a question
I couldn't have asked.

'Love notes,' she decides.
'Myths broken as well as lives
and dreams.'

Wow! I think, and Gail slowly
nods her head and
pushes the alien
poster aside.

As Gail rips out a page
with tomato soup cans
then shreds them into mosaic
pieces, she talks.
'Steve's dreams are in pieces here,
as are Mum's and my sister's.'
Cas slides to the floor
and opens another magazine.
'Some of this milky white
of the Actil sheet ad would be
good for the cow and love notes.

Just like Tyson,' she adds.
'His life is changed.
I wish my love notes would
fix up his problems.'

And Gail quietly
talks about Steve,
weaving the words
of his short life
into the creases
and texture
of the poster,
as we cut,
rip,
paste
and follow
Gail's directions.

How the extraordinary becomes ordinary

On Monday after school,
Gail and I are waiting
at the bus stop; seems
like a large part of high school
is waiting, waiting.

We are chatting about Saturday
about collage, colours, texture.
Gail is a natural with artwork
and I'm in awe.
Then Cas comes up,
she looks happy
and Tyson is with her.

'This is Tyson.'
Cas bends
her hand towards
her boyfriend.
I nod.

Tyson looks at Gail.
'Was your brother
in Vietnam?'
he asks.

'Yes,' nods Gail, as if
she's been waiting

to be asked this question
for a long time.
'Cas told me your brother
was a conscript.'
I hear him talking softly
to Gail. 'Same as me.
Wish I'd met him.
He was killed, wasn't he?
Tell me about him.'

And Gail talks about Steve
about her little sister,
about her mum
and how unhappy
she is and how
no one seems
to understand
their family's pain.
She says, 'Some
neighbours look
at us as if we've done
something awful.
No one asks about Steve
and some turn away
to avoid us.
I hate it.'

I stare up at the sky,
watching a little plane
droning its way across

the afternoon sky,
weaving in and out of
white tear-apart clouds.

We stand there, listening,
as a bond grows between Gail
and Tyson, all because of war.
Cas listens, nods,
reaches for Tyson's
hand and holds it.

Gail's bus pulls up,
she gives a little wave
and walks up the first
step. She holds her head
up a bit more as if a
weight of words
has loosened the burden
she has been hugging tight.

Posters, for good, for trouble, for hiding

Cas is still hiding
rolled-up posters
behind her
dressing table.
She's pushed the dressing
table right against the wall.

The posters balance
in the middle,
resting on the bolt
that holds the mirror
to the table.

I see
the curl of posters,
a glimpse of a person
behind bars,
words like:
Two years jail
End conscription.
Then another poster
with barbed wire
around a baby's feet.
Ugh! I don't like that.
I squirm.

Is this what Tyson
has seen?
Or Gail's brother Steve?

Later, Jules is chasing
a mouse: the old walls
and ceilings are perfect
palaces for rodents
when the weather
gets cooler.

Jules is skittering
along the edges
of the hallway
and into our
bedroom.

The cat jumps onto
the dressing table.
Whoosh, go the bottles,
the brushes, the hairclips,
then away runs the mouse
behind the dressing table.

Jules follows, dislodges
those secretive posters,
unrolling them across
the bedroom rug
like an invasion

from outer space,
outer time.

'Ooh!' I squeal,
and know I need
to re-hide those posters.
But all the noise brings Cas
and Mum and Dad.

'Did you—' begins Cas,
accusing me.
Then sees my cat
coming from behind
the dressing table
with the mouse,
a thin straggle
of cobwebs
on Jules's back.

'What's all this noise about?
And *what* are these?'
demands Dad, as he bends
to pick up the posters.

I sit on my bed,
wishing I could pull
my quilt over my head.
Cas has
bright red cheeks.

'Where did these come from?
Cas? Sharnie?'
Dad is unrolling the posters,
then he looks right
at Cas. She has tears
in her eyes.

'I thought I told you before
to get rid of these.
Don't you listen to me?'
Dad is getting red
in the face, too.

'This sort of propaganda
undermines what our
brave soldiers have fought
for in other wars. Our freedom!'
Dad growls.

'How could you, Cas?' wails Mum.

'I'll tell you why,' Cas says.
'They're not telling
us the truth about this war.
It stinks. It's evil.
Look what they're doing.
Can't you see?'

Cas points to
the baby on the poster.

'That's real, not the stuff
they're saying
in the newspapers!
Ask one of the returned
soldiers about the truth!'

Cas runs from the room
in a welter of tears.

Dad takes the posters
and looks like he is about
to burn them in the kitchen
stove, or even shred them
to bits, like he did
with the other poster,
but stops
and flings them
back into our bedroom.

'I want them out of the house
by the time I come back,'
he says,
and slams the back door
as he goes outside to the shed.
There is no arguing with Dad
when he gives
an ultimatum like that.

As it grows dark,
I look through the window

and see the moon sailing
through and around
clouds heavy with rain,
as if it's trying to mend
the rents
in the night sky.
A constant glow,
dim, then bright,
then like a pearl
in a stormy oyster
of night.

If there was
a man in the moon,
then he should be
protesting about Earth's
invasion of his territory.
And then I think,
it's like our nation
invading another country
killing, destroying.
If I was asked my opinion
now, I'd be with Cas.

But no one's asking
and our house feels
like a war zone.
Everyone seems angry,
sad, sorry and not talking.
Dad is so furious.

He tells us at dinner
that Grandpa would be
disappointed that a
granddaughter of his
was a protestor.

But I know Grandma
would be on Cas's side.
I need to tell Cas
what Grandma said.

Gail, come quickly … please

'Cas,' I begin, standing outside
our closed bedroom door,
'there's something
you should know.'
'Go away,' shouts Cas.
'Why doesn't everyone
leave me ALONE!'

I wait,
unsure what to do next,
and that's when the sharp
sad muffled crying begins.
I turn and go outside.

I need help
or advice.
I miss
Grandma,
but there is
another person
who can help.

When the phone
is answered, I say,
'Is Gail there, please?'
I grip the receiver
when an abrupt voice says,

‘Who’s this?’
‘It’s Sharnie, her friend.’

The phone is put down,
I can hear footsteps
on the other end
and someone calling, ‘Gaillll!
For you, phone call.’

‘Sharnie?’ Gail’s voice
in the distance
is squeaky,
high,
excited.
Then she says more quietly,
‘Hello,’ into the receiver.
‘Um, Gail,’ I say.
I have to stop
my voice from
becoming watery,
how dare it.

I swallow
and whisper,
‘It’s Cas,
I don’t know what to do …’

‘Coming.’
Just like that Gail says,
‘I’m coming over.

Oh, I'll bring one
of our posters
to show Cas how
much we've done.'

I cringe at the word
'poster' but Gail
is the one who might just
know what to do.
Might show me
a way into Cas's
feelings, just
maybe.

I'm like an astronaut
about to step into
the deep unknown.
Will my footprint sink
without a trace,
or will I walk closer
to Cas?

All I know is that I need
someone else to be here,
to talk me through
a new frontier.

Mending, moonbeams and moon dreams

When Gail comes
we sit outside
in the backyard.
I whisper to Gail
about the hidden posters
and barbed wire
and trust and parents
and Grandma and Lewis.
The words are spilling
like grains of potting mix,
but Gail just nods
and strokes Jules.

Something makes me
stop mid-sentence.
Gail is looking at Cas,
she is holding the back door
open wide.

'Come in,' she says.
Cas is blowing her nose
and her voice is all
washed out.
I hesitate, look at Cas.
'Come on,' she says.
I'm coming.

Gail and I both see
red welts
like someone's
been scratching
Cas's eyes with prickles.

Cas blows her nose
again,
tosses the tissue
into the already full bin.
She clears her throat
and says, 'Good to see
you, Gail,'
but her eyes
acknowledge me also.

Gail looks at me
and nods. I feel
I am in the space
capsule *Eagle*
about to leave
the main rocket,
no turning back,
but going forward.
I am moonwalking
to Cas.

'Cas,' I have taken
the first step. 'Cas,'

I repeat: it's so hard
this moonwalking.

I take a big gulp of air
and stride out further
with my words.
I am about to plant
that flag on
the moon's surface.
I have to reach Cas.

I say, 'Grandma knew about
you marching in the protest.
She said she would have
done that, too.'

Cas looks at me,
really looks at me
and smiles.
Gail speaks up then.
'Um, Cas, I got
to know Tyson
a bit after you
introduced us.
He came around
to see my mum and sister …'
She pauses.

Cas nods and Gail continues.
'He told me a few things,

he's been applying for jobs,
but the minute he writes
down his service
in Vietnam,
he's shoved
to the bottom of the list.
Imagine that!
He also said he needs
space to clear up
everything in his head,
the world looks so different,
he said, this side of his Vietnam
War service.'

Cas nods and opens
her hand to show a tightly
folded note.
'He said the same to me.'
And she starts to softly cry.

Gail and I stand
awkwardly, so much
for bravely taking moon steps;
we're frozen to the spot.

Cas blows her nose for
the umpteenth time
and points to Gail.
'What have you got there?'

Gail releases the posters
from under her arm.

'I brought this one for you,
and this one to show you
what we've done since you last
saw the poster.'

I butt in now, 'And to talk
about what we plan to do
at the school space display.'

'I'm not sure …'
begins Cas as she
takes in the poster.
But in one swish
our bedroom
is transformed
into an outer space
experience.
It's the poster Gail
discarded
of an astronaut
looking
over
the lip of the moon
to the Earth below
and saying, *'I can see*
the carnage of the

Vietnam War
from here.'

'Wow!'

'It's all Gail's artwork,' I say.

'You sure can draw, Gail.'
Cas lifts the poster
to an empty space
above her bed.

Gail stands back and looks.
I poke Cas and she nods.
'It's just that Dad has a thing
about posters
and the Vietnam War,
so how about we
change the caption
to something like …'
She breaks off, thinking hard.

I know, so I say, 'Maybe something
like: *Earth, I can't find any moon cheese,*
but there is a Sea of Tranquility
that you need NOW!'

'Yes!' shouts Gail.
'It still has a message,

but has humour too.
What do you think, Cas?'

Cas nods
and Gail finds
a piece of paper
to cover her message
from the little cachet
of paper she's brought
with her.

'Clever you,' Cas squeezes
me in a quick hug,
releases me slowly,
says, 'Can you help me
with a poster or two
for the protest
we have planned?'

Her voice is very small,
but it's just the opening
I need. 'Well Gail and I
are thinking of making the
school showcase a way we can
protest the war. We're hoping
our poster wins or gets
an honourable mention,
we want to be interviewed
by the newspaper reporter.

So we can help,
right, Gail?'

Gail nods and smiles,
'What do you have in mind,
Cas?'

It's real, it's both gloriously sad and happy

The whole world
is talking, listening,
reading
and at last watching
on a black-and-white TV.

Lewis pops in whenever
he can and says,
'We have lift-off!'
He does a countdown
of a rocket searing
into space and is building
his own *Apollo 11*
out of anything he can
find in Mum's kitchen
or Dad's garage.
'Don't forget to ask
first,' I whisper to him.

Of an evening everyone
waits for the news, for the
special moon reports.
If they can't watch
it at home, they go
down to the electrical
goods shop and watch

the TVs set up along
the shopfront windows.

On Friday
the announcement
crackled over
the loudspeaker:
'Man on the moon,
view and be part
of history.
Two TV sets
will be available
to watch
in the home domestic rooms,
the largest spaces in the school,
but if you can
watch it at home, then do
so, you have permission
to go home at lunch break,
just bring a note from your parents,'
says Mr Grear.

I think of Grandma,
how she would have loved
this moment, wondering
about those three astronauts
training, working, waiting,
praying that they will do
what President Kennedy

predicted all those years ago:
to land a man on the moon
and bring him home again.

Lewis and I would have
sat with Grandma, sipped tea,
munched on her peanut brittle
and wondered at rocket
power, ingenuity, telescopes,
communication from Earth
to moon.

Where is my communication
to you, Grandma?
Then a picture of her
garden comes to mind,
of her potplants
thriving into new life
and I don't feel
quite so sad.

21 July 1969

On Monday, after an early
lunchbreak, I go to the home
domestic room.
It feels like a holiday,
unstructured, like the whole
world is holding its breath.

Will man land on the moon?
Or will there be a problem,
a disaster? What will they
find there? Will my little
world change? Will the
moon suddenly change colour
or disappear?
I still think about this,
even though we've learnt
so much about the moon.
I wanted to watch
the moon landing
at school, to be with Gail,
share it with her.

Gail has saved me a seat.
It's hard to see the little
TV box, but its full of magic,
wonder, suspense.

I feel a hand on my shoulder,
Cas squeezes it as she sits
behind us with her friends.
We watch the screen
as 1pm arrives. We
strain forward
as Neil Armstrong
climbs down the ladder
backwards from *Eagle*
and places
his foot on the moon.

Gail and I hug.
It's momentous!
Everyone is talking,
clapping,
then words crackle out,
with gaps of silence between
them. We all instinctively hush:

*'That's one small step for man
one giant leap for mankind.'*

Moonlight from the conquered moon

That night
Lewis comes over,
he is so excited.
We switch off
the lights inside
and sit out on the lawn
in the darkness.
Mum and Dad
have a torch
and Cas lights
a candle a little way off.

The stars are spread
out like a ceremonial
shawl, so bright,
so far away.

Lewis has a little toy
telescope; he points it
to the moon. 'Can't see
the *Apollo 11* spaceship.'
He relays the information
to me as if I am the Parkes
tracking station.
'The moon looks the same
as it did last night.'

I laugh because I know
how useless that telescope
is – it used to be mine when
I was younger.

Lewis turns the telescope
on me and fires a question:
'So where did the *Eagle* land
on the moon?'

'The Sea of Tranquility,'
I say.

But that sets me wondering,
is it tranquil on the moon
with footprints that will
never blow away?

Then I suddenly think,
at least we're not at war
with the man in the moon.

Planting, but will it grow?

For several days after the moon
landing, we re-watch the footprint
moment, every news bulletin
starts with it,
then see Buzz Aldrin
plant a flag and plaque
on the moon's surface.

I think of space explorers
and how the moon
is no longer mysterious,
or silver, but conquered
with a flag and plaque.
Aldrin's footprints
will last forever.
Will Grandma's footprint
last that long?
It will,
It will,
in here,
in my heart.

I think again
of the photo of Neil Armstrong
on the front cover
of the newspapers
and the TV shots

as he climbed down the
Eagle ladder, before stepping
onto the moon's surface.
Was his heart racing with fear?
Just like Gail's brother Steve
as he went to Vietnam?

They both would have thought
of not coming back
from such missions.
But one would always be a hero,
the other quickly forgotten.

How can we look up
and touch the moon,
when we don't know how
to look across to our neighbours
to listen and take note
of their opinions?

I think of Cas
of Mum
of Dad
of Gail.
Then Grandma.
Oh, Grandma.

Poster heaven or poster hell?

Our posters are on display
all along the school corridor,
and there, in bold colours
and collaged with segments
of breakfast cereal advertisements,
pages of the *Women's Weekly*
and silver foil from
the milk bottle tops,
is our alien creature poster
and our cow and nursery
rhyme poster.

Clusters of students
dawdle down the corridor,
pointing,
choosing what they like best.

Cas's friends call over
to Gail and me.
'We love your poster,
so zany and bright!'
'Thanks,' we say
and give each other
a mini-hug.
Ellie, Marg and Mia
deliberately walk our way,
humming a little song

about aliens in green suits
and mutter about *Lost in Space*,
the TV show everyone
wants to watch on a Friday night.

Gail whispers about people
being lost in the here and now.
As we walk along and look
at the huge variety
of posters we try to pick
one that could rival ours.

Mr Grear enters the corridor
with two newspaper journalists,
as well as the head of the school
council. There are a few chairs
set up where the corridor widens
and branches off into three
smaller corridors of
classrooms and lockers.

'Attention please, everyone.'
Miss Parkes ushers
the students into lines
as Mr Grear begins
to announce the winners
and give a little spiel about the school.
One newspaper journalist
clicks Mr Grear with his arms wide,
but then the orderly line

is pushed apart
and Cas and her friends
don sandwich boards
and hold up the posters Gail,
Cas and I designed.

There is a shocked silence,
The whole audience turns.

Stop this war,
Save conscripts' lives.
No bombs can bring
peace.

The reporters click cameras,
Mr Grear's arms are
stuck in space.

When he recovers from the shock
he says, sternly but firmly,
'Please leave your protest
boards and return to the general
student body.'

The protestors don't move.
My legs somehow walk towards
Cas and I hold her hand.
She gives it a squeeze and I see
what a brave face Cas
has plastered on.

Gail quickly follows and links hands
with me and one of Cas's friends,
then other students break away
and link hands and arms – a
picket fence of human flesh –
until there is just a small pocket
of students looking on, shocked,
Ellie, Marg and Mia among
their number.

Mr Grear looks flustered,
the head of the school council
looks grim-faced,
but the principal plows on,
and I have a grudging respect
for him.
'I will now continue on with
the announcement of
of the space poster contest:
second place goes to Gail Long
and Sharnie Burley.'

There are whoops
of joy and clapping,
the picket line drops hands
and we become students again.
Then the winner is announced
and I heave a sigh of relief;
it isn't Ellie and her mob,
but an art student

from Cas's form level.
'Dismissed,' says Mr Grear abruptly,
but Miss Parkes has
tapped several of us
on the shoulder.

'Follow me,' she says.
But a reporter interrupts her:
'Can we have a line
or two from you?'

Gail freezes, the Gail who
is usually brave and outspoken.

I open my mouth and say:
'Gail's brother Steve was a conscript
in this Vietnam War and died.
We dedicate our poster to him.'

Afterwards, is there change?

The newspaper is thrown
on our breakfast table.
There is Gail and there is
me, pointing to our
second-prize poster
with my words in bold font beneath.
Dad is glowering at me,
not Cas, but me …

'I'd expect Cas to be in the thick
of this protest, but you, Sharnie?
Do you know how much this hurts
your mother and me?
What would Grandma think?'

Dad doesn't expect me to answer
but I do.
'She would think it was great
that I have a mind of my own.
She didn't like war either.'
Mum gasps, then slowly nods.
Cas is beside me, holding my hand.

Dad's shoulders sag, 'This war
is a mess,' he agrees,
'but you've disobeyed all
of the warnings I've given you

and now you'll be grounded
for the next few weeks
as punishment.
Lucky you weren't expelled
from school.'

I know that's because there
wouldn't have been many students
left to teach,
but I don't point this out to Dad.
'I want to see you
put all your creative energy
into your schoolwork now.
And, Cas,' Dad says,
looking directly at her,
'none of this boyfriend nonsense
alright? There will be plenty
of time at home to think about
your actions and consequences.'

Cas sighs. 'Tyson is going anyway,'
she says in a small voice. 'He's going
to find work up north at a new mine …
You know, Dad, he couldn't get work
here—'
But Dad puts up a hand.
'Enough, Cas.'

We leave Mum and Dad
together in the kitchen

and go back to our sanctuary,
our bedroom.

'I can't get over
you coming to hold my hand,'
Cas says, 'I didn't know what else
we could do once we stood there
with our sandwich boards.
I hadn't thought that far ahead.'
She gives me a quick hug.
'Doesn't seem to have helped
stop the war,' she says sadly.
'Just made a mess with Dad
and Mum and at school.
And now Tyson's going.'

'Oh, Cas,' I hug her. 'It has made
a big difference. Look at Gail,
look at me,' and I laugh.

Twists and turns

Gail calls me on the phone
and it's me twirling the cord
around my arm as I sit
at our special telephone table
and matching chair. Jules
is a good substitute for fluffy
slippers as she sits at my feet.

'I'm missing school,' Gail says.
'Never thought I'd be
saying that!
I'm missing you too, Sharnie.'
I agree, then wait as Gail
tells me her news.
'Tyson called us.
He's off to find work
elsewhere, a new start,
he said. He brought
my sister a kite he'd made.
It has a scene of a Vietnam
rice paddy on it.
And he told us about
the jungles, and a little
bit about the war.
Mum listened, too,
even smiled when Tyson
told us he hadn't painted

since primary school.
He says he paints a bit now,
helps him sort things out
in his head. He even
brought us a sample
of Vietnamese food
he's learned to cook.
It was certainly different
but Mum asked about a recipe.
Haven't heard her ask
anything like that for a while.'

I murmur and make comments:
'Really? That's great, Gail.'
Then she runs out of steam.
'You'll have to come over
and cheer Cas up with news
of Tyson,' I suggest.

'How about this Saturday?'
she says.
I agree and we say goodbye.

That night Mum
hands me a little bundle
marked:
Sharnie, for your glory box.

She gives me a little smile
and hugs me. She whispers,

'Grandma would be proud
of you, Sharnie.'

Before she goes back
to the kitchen I ask,
'What's a glory box?'
'Ah, a glory box,
that's a special container,
could be a chest,
to hold treasure
for your future home-
making.'

I look puzzled,
so Mum adds,
'For when
you get married.
Everyone in Grandma's time
always sewed
or saved for little things
for their own home,
like tea towels,
tablecloths,
salt-and-pepper shakers.'

Hmm. I feel the package.
It's wrapped
in an apron of Grandma's.
I gently unwind
little crocheted doilies,

Grandma's knitting needles,
wool and a cookery book
all jiggled together.

Then a slip of paper drops out.
Sharnie, my secateurs
are in the laundry
and the shells and
special stones I gathered
are in there as well.
You'll know what to do.
My own grandmother
had green fingers, too.

An idea, a confession

Gail comes on Saturday;
she hands me a card
and smiles.
'Sorry it's late,
a lot going on lately.'
Gail has drawn
a huge bunch of flowers.
'It's lovely,' I say,
and my throat
feels tight.
'My grandma would
have loved that,'
I tell her,
and then sniff
to try to keep
back tears
as I blurt out
a question.
'Gail, is it okay
to keep thinking
about things
I could have done
for Grandma,
but now it's too late?'

I want to recall the words
as soon as I've said them,

but Gail sits a bit closer now
and whispers, 'I think
of lots of things I could
have said to my brother.
We did have goodbyes
before he left for Vietnam,
and now when I see his bike
or his empty bedroom,
I wish I could
have said more.
It's okay, Sharnie.
It took me a while
to stop thinking
like that every day.'

I'm glad Gail's told me
this. I never would have
thought I'd ask Gail
or anyone a question
like that.
But Gail tells me more.

'Sad part is Mum
thinks Steve's
missing in action
and he'll surprise us
by walking through
the door one day.
It's hard to keep
the house normal

and my sister happy.
It's like Mum
is missing in action.
My father died years ago,
so it's just me to watch
over everything. Ha!
You know I forget
to bring lunch most days.'

We just sit there quietly
for a while. I still think
Grandma might be really
at home, in her garden,
that she's not dead at all.
And that gives me an idea.
I need to talk to Cas first.

A plot, some rosemary

Cas is helping me,
'Good idea, Sharnie.'
Lewis is helping too.
'It doesn't have to be a big
area,' I say, 'just enough
for Mum and Dad and Gail's
family to plant these
rosemary bushes.'

I told Gail about my idea
and she pointed out
that on Anzac Day,
her mum often picks a sprig
of rosemary to pin to her coat.
'To remember Steve,
to say we still love him.'
She is helping, too,
using her art skills, designing
the small planting area with us.

'Will they all come?' Lewis asks
as he squirts a cabbage moth
with his space gun.
'Of course, and Cas and I have baked.'
Lewis races to the back porch
of Grandma's house.

We have the teacups, the teapot
and two plates of Grandma's slice,
cooked by us. 'And peanut brittle,'
says Lewis, rubbing his tummy.

'Go and stand by the gate,'
I say to Lewis.
'They're coming,' Lewis yells.
Cas, Gail and I stand up, brush soil
off our jeans and watch
as Dad opens Grandma's gate
for Gail's mum and sister.

Dad is saying,
'I'm sorry about your son
Steve,' and Gail's sister
is admiring Lewis's space gun.

Everyone stands around
the little heart-shaped
garden we've dug
in Grandma's lawn.
We will plant the cuttings
Lewis and I potted
with Grandma …
ages ago I think.

Cas hands Gail a rosemary plant.
Gail kneels, as does her mum

and little sister. Then Cas
gives Gail a little wooden
plaque. *In memory of Steve
Long, a Vietnam conscript.*
'Not like the moon
plaque,' pipes up Lewis,
and everyone laughs and the
tension is broken.

As Mum and Dad
plant a rosemary bush
Cas hands them a plaque.
*In memory of our dear mother
and grandmother.*

We are silent
just looking
at the little garden we've made.
Dad says, 'Well done girls,
and you too Lewis'.

'There's more,' yells Lewis,
'tea and toffee.'
Then he shares one of those
amazing moon facts
he knows: 'At least there
will be wind here to blow
through the rosemary bushes.
No wind on the moon.'

And we laugh again.
Mum takes Gail's mum for
a walk around Grandma's garden,
and Gail says, 'This was a great idea,
Sharnie. Mum seems almost like
her normal self today. See,
you've got your own special
talent.'

The last of the posters

'About those posters,' begins Gail,
and Cas and I groan.
'Well, you said last time
that we have to tie up loose ends,
and here I am.
I've brought my magic
artwork hands with me.'

We smile as Gail raises
her hands above her head
like an orchestra conductor
tapping attention, ready
for the music to begin.

'It will be the last time I attempt
a poster,' says Cas firmly.
'We're finally doing what Dad
wants.'

'Not me,' asserts Gail.
'I reckon I could design covers
for records or do advertising
signs.'

'But for now,' says Gail, as she
flips the first of Cas's Vietnam

War posters over,
'for now, for you, Cas,
how about fluffy slippers,
a box of toffee at your elbow
and you holding the telephone
with the long cord curling
around you?'

And with a few strokes Gail
has Cas looking like Cas,
smiling like Cas,
my sister Cas.

'Sharnie?' muses Gail
as the second poster
is turned over ready
for a new drawing.
'Hmm, how about
the moon and Lewis's
space gun, Jules hiding
from Lewis in a garden
full of pots and colour,
your Grandma's
garden of course.'

Gail makes the moon
so big,
sailing above
a garden full of colour,

and a tiny Lewis
armed, ready to fire
at an alien.

Gail startles us
by saying, 'Now, I want
to trace around
your feet.
Only one foot each though.
Your right foot, Cas,
then Sharnie's slightly behind,
then mine.'

'There,' she says.
'Our footprints on the moon.'

It's like an unspoken
promise to each other,
right now as we
sit on Cas's bed and think
of the future.

Gail draws a little heart
in one corner of the poster.
For Steve, she writes.
Cas draws a heart
in the opposite corner.
For Tyson, she writes.

Then Cas turns to me.
'Who's your heart going
to be for?'

My heart is still
full of Grandma
so I write her name.

It feels like a letting go,
these posters,
these hearts,
this friend,
this sister.

I am close to tears
when Jules jumps
through the open window
and we squeal in shock.

Then a smidgeon
of the old Cas says,
'I've got an idea.
I have spare change
in my piggy bank.
Let's go get
a milkshake or chips.
Come on.'

'It's a bit of a walk,'
I half-protest.
But not really;
I need a walk.

As I turn back and
look at the poster
I say a silent prayer:
Moon, we've left our footprints, too.
I know that your moon dust won't
blow them away.
Not yet … not yet.

Acknowledgements

Always thanks to my husband Kelvin, and my big family who cheer me on in different ways.

Thank you to Kristina Schultz who first contracted my story and loved it, to Vanessa Pellatt who began untangling my plot threads and offering suggestions, to Clair Hume who supported me, offered advice and encouragement – I always need encouragement! Many thanks to Kristy Bushnell who showed me ways to make Sharnie shine on her own moonbeam and lastly to Jacqueline Blanchard who polished the final version. Thanks Kate Wong for a great cover, Jo Hunt for the book design and all others behind the scenes at UQP. Lastly, to Jane Novak my agent who always offers support.

This story has been undergoing transformations for a number of years, always as a verse novel but with many episodes altered, deleted and rewritten. Many times it seemed like this story would be aborted like an epic space mission, but if nothing else I've learned grit and perseverance, and always kept faith that this story needs to be shared with a new generation.

A verse novel can carry the girders of great emotion and give us glimpses of poetry that is universally inspired through space, through history itself.